The Marble Cliffs

...rest

Mount Wyrd

e Bilious Bog

Fola Dubh Mountains

Gypsum-upon-Swathmud

y Forest
Hollow

Ande-Dubnos
home of the Sluagh Horde

Hollow Hills

A Dreadful
Fairy Book

A Dreadful Fairy Book

NARRATED BY
Quentin Q. Quacksworth, Esq.

WRITTEN BY
Jon Etter

WITH ILLUSTRATIONS BY
Adam Horsepool

AMBERJACK
PUBLISHING

IDAHO

AMBERJACK
PUBLISHING

Amberjack Publishing
1472 E. Iron Eagle Drive
Eagle, ID 83616
amberjackpublishing.com

Library of Congress Cataloging-in-Publication Data

Names: Etter, Jon, author. | Horsepool, Adam, 1992- illustrator.
Title: A dreadful fairy book : narrated by Quentin Q. Quacksworth, Esq. / written by Jon Etter ; with illustrations by Adam Horsepool.
Description: New York ; Idaho : Amberjack Publishing, [2018] | Summary: Shade, a sassy sprite, never fit in at her village, so when her treehouse burns down she sets out to find a new home and, with luck, others who love books and learning.
Identifiers: LCCN 2018037009 (print) | LCCN 2018043147 (ebook) | ISBN 9781948705271 (ebook) | ISBN 9781948705141 (hardcover : alk. paper)
Subjects: | CYAC: Fairies--Fiction. | Adventure and adventurers--Fiction. | Books and reading--Fiction. | Friendship--Fiction. | Humorous stories.
Classification: LCC PZ7.1.E856 (ebook) | LCC PZ7.1.E856 Dr 2018 (print) | DDC [Fic]--dc23
LC record available at https://lccn.loc.gov/2018037009

ISBN: 978-1-948705-14-1
E-ISBN: 978-1-948705-27-1

10 9 8 7 6 5 4 3 2 1

"If you're ever lost in a strange place, find a library and go in."

—ADVICE GIVEN TO THE AUTHOR
WHEN HE WAS A BOY BY HIS MOTHER,
CONSTANCE ETTER

FROM JON:

To Nikki, Evelyn, and Jack: This book and the fulfillment of my childhood dream to someday have a book sitting on a shelf in a library would never have happened if it weren't for you. I love you all so much.

FROM QUACKSWORTH:

To nobody, for I don't believe it healthy or proper to despise anyone so much that one would dedicate this dreadful tome to them.

· PREFACE ·

A Warning from the Narrator

What you hold in your hands is a dreadful fairy book. Please allow me to explain.

First, by fairy story standards, this story is quite dreadful. While most stories involving sprites, pixies, brownies, elves, trolls, goblins, and all other manner of fairy folk are quite delightful and whimsical, filled with adventure, and teach all sorts of wonderful lessons about the importance of friendship and helpfulness and the healing power of clapping one's hands, this story has very little of any of those things.

Second, the fairies in this story are quite dreadful at *being* fairies. While there are some nasty fairy types throughout that are, in fact, very nasty—thus meeting our nasty fairy expectations—others that should be nasty are actually uncharacteristically (and disappointingly) nice. Even worse, many of the fairies that are supposed to be kind and helpful and friendly are, more often than not, exceedingly surly, dishonest, and generally unpleasant company, and the main lesson one can learn from them is "Try to keep better company than these folks." In truth, good Reader, I wish I could narrate for you almost any other fairy story than this one. Sadly, my alarm clock did not go off the day that storytelling assignments were given, and this was about all that was left. But I am a professional narrator and this is my lot, so I will tell this dreadful story as undreadfully as I possibly can.

Your Humble
Narrator,
Quentin Q. Quacksworth, Esq.
UNITED FEDERATION OF NARRATORS, RACONTEURS, ANECDOTISTS, AND GENERAL TELLERS OF TALES, LOCAL 42

In which a sprite's home is burned,
fairies are yelled at, and rude
language is used . . .

T ears rolled down Shade's chubby, chestnut-brown
cheeks as she watched the sprites of Pleasant
Hollow, their butterfly wings all the colors of the
rainbow, fly back and forth between the crystal blue
spring that supplied their tiny village with water and
the hollow tree that was her home. Her neighbors tried
valiantly, but futilely, to put out the raging flames that

consumed her little home. Bucket after bucket of water they splashed onto the tree but to little effect—the wood was too dry, too dead, and the flames too hot, too fierce for them to do more than contain the fire to that one single tree. When they were done, all that was left was smoldering rubble, which Shade poked at miserably with a stick, hoping that something she loved might've survived the flames.

Amidst the black and gray ruins of her home, she spied a small patch of red. Her heart quickened. *My book!* she thought, quickly clearing ash to reveal a charred but mostly intact rectangle of red leather. Snatching up the book cover, Shade's heart sank when she discovered that was all it was: just a cover, the pages within having burned up in the fire. Shade turned it over. On the scorched inside cover, Shade could only read a few words of the inscription she had long ago memorized after reading it every day of her life since she first learned how to read:

Our Dear Little Shade,

While all the books of this house belong to all of us, as most books should, this one will be yours and yours alone because everyone should have one book that especially belongs to them. Keep it and cherish it and always remember: No matter how alone you may feel, books will always be your friends.

Love always and forever,
Mom and Dad

Shade wiped away her tears and began to frantically sift through the rest of the nearby rubble, hoping desperately that some other book from her collection had survived. Eventually she found one, charred and soggy but intact. Written in gold leaf on its blue cover were the words *Traveling in the Greater Kingdom: A Guide to the Wonders and Dangers of the Fairy World by Stinkletoe Radishbottom.*

Shade hugged it to her chest and wept, thinking of all that she had lost: her mother, lost when she went off to fight in a war that everyone in Pleasant Hollow said was none of their concern; her father, lost to the blight that ravaged the hollow some seventeen seasons ago; and now her books—*The Adventures of Hagan Finnegan, Gigglings and Titterings, Good Governess Jane,* and all the rest, including *her* book—to a stupid, stupid fire.

With a fluttering of vibrant orange and yellow wings, Pleasant Hollow's chieftainess, Sungleam Flutterglide, alighted gracefully next to Shade and placed her hand on Shade's shoulder. "I'm sorry," she declared loud enough for all to hear. "We did what we could."

As she said this, the other fairies of the hollow alighted and crowded around, doing their best to look sympathetic and kind, as they waited for Shade to say something. The red, orange, and yellow autumn leaves above their heads rustled in the breeze as Shade stared at the ground, silent. The silence grew increasingly awkward, and the assembled sprites exchanged uneasy glances until Shade said in a choked whisper, "Did what you could . . ."

"Yes, Lillyshadow Glitterdemalion, we did," Chieftainess Flutterglide replied. She then smiled a smile filled with optimism and good cheer and very white teeth. "And now we will do all we can. We, all of us, will build you a new and better home!"

A cheer went up amongst all the sprites. *Yes!* they all agreed. *We will indeed make her a better home, and all will be right with the world! It will be a Grand Project!* They all dearly loved Grand Projects. As the sprites congratulated themselves on their kindness and helpfulness and ingenuity, Shade wiped the tears from her eyes and gazed at the crowd.

Now, if this were a proper fairy book, this is the point where Shade would be overcome with gratitude and realize what wonderful friends and neighbors she had and how, in spite of losing her home and almost all of her worldly belongings, she was truly fortunate indeed. But, as I warned you in the preface, this is not a proper fairy book but a *dreadful* one.

"You . . . You . . . utter rockheads!" Shade bellowed. "You grub-sucking, slime-licking mudbrains!"

Chieftainess Flutterglide looked confused. "Um, Lillyshadow, I—"

"It's 'Shade,' you termite-kisser. *Shade!* How many times do I have to tell you slack-jawed halfwits?"

Flutterglide held up her hands as if to ward off Shade's anger. "Look, Lillyshadow, I know you're upset but—"

"Shade. It's *Shade.* And you're dingle-dangle right I'm upset."

A few of the sprites gasped, and parents in the crowd clapped their hands over the ears of their children. "Language!" one of them gasped.

"She said the D word," a young sprite giggled. "And the other D word!"

"You burned down my house!" Shade shouted.

The chieftainess frowned. "Now, that was an accident, Lillyshadow. How could any of us know that something like this would happen?"

Shade took a step forward, the hand not clutching Radishbottom's book balled up into a fist, and glared up at Chieftainess Flutterglide, who was a full head taller than her. "How could you know, you clod? How could you know that setting off *fireworks*—which, when lit, spew *fire*—in the middle of a *forest*, which is made of *wood*, which *burns when set on fire*, could cause a *fire*?"

Flutterglide nodded. "Exactly. The two traveling fairies we bought them from said they were perfectly safe. How could we know—?"

"Maybe if a single one of you had ever read a single page in a single book in your entire dingle-dangle lives, you'd have the single ounce of sense it takes not to set off jets of flame near your *wooden* homes. Especially in autumn!"

The sprites all gave each other knowing glances and shook their heads. *Books!* Shade's father, Fernshadow Featherfall, had spent his entire life trying to convince the residents of Pleasant Hollow that they ought to waste precious time that could be spent merrymaking or playing acorn-toss or working on Grand Projects and instead spend their time reading from musty collections of paper moldering away in their rotting old tree, just as his father had done before him, and his father before him. The chieftainess smiled a patient smile. "But it's all right, Lillyshadow. We'll make you a *new* house. A *better* one!"

"A better one?" She thought of the home that she had just lost. Yes, the wood was gray and rotted in places, and, yes, it got damp when it rained—and, she had to admit, a little stinky—and, yes, it was drafty and cold in the winter, but it was where she had grown up. It had held all of her family keepsakes, and, most importantly, it had housed the books that her family had cared for for many generations. She snorted and spat at the ground in front of Flutterglide. "That's what I think of your new house and this whole dingle-dangle village. I'm taking my book and I'm leaving!"

As she stormed off, Flutterglide called after her, "But where will you go?"

Without turning, Shade shouted, "Anywhere that's away from you sap-headed termite-kissers. Get donkled!"

"She just said the other, other D word!" the same little sprite as before giggled. "The worst one!"

The sprites of Pleasant Hollow stared as Shade stomped off into the Merry Forest. While they all felt a little bit bad about burning down Shade's house and parting on such poor terms with her, they also felt a great deal of relief—Shade and her family's bookish ways and tendency to ask questions and "know things" and generally ruin their fun had always been such a nuisance. And none of them especially cared for being called "termite-kissers" or "mud-brains."

"So," the chieftainess piped up cheerily once Shade was gone, "Shall we build a house?"

"Oh, yes!" the sprites cried and fluttered off, happily throwing themselves into a Grand Project, unconcerned in the least where Shade might be going or what she might encounter along the way.

In which Shade meets an Anthony
o' the Wisp and settles on a vague
course of action . . .

I n a blind rage over losing her house because of the
stupid and reckless actions of the rather empty-
headed residents of the village where she had spent
her entire life, Shade crunched through the dry autumn leaves of the forest for hours before realizing that
she didn't know where she was headed.

Now, kind Reader, you are probably wondering,

"Why is Shade walking? She's a sprite—a winged spe-cies of fairy—so shouldn't she be flying?" My answer to that very astute question, which, I must say, does a won-derful job of displaying your vast knowledge of fairies and their tales, is this: Shade, being a fairly dreadful fairy, didn't like to fly. She wasn't very good at it (mostly due to lack of practice, energy, and interest, although she usually blamed it on being a good deal shorter and chubbier, and therefore less aerodynamic, than the vast majority of sprites—a fact that was regularly and cruelly pointed out to her growing up), plus it made her tummy feel wobbly, so she walked whenever she could.

Eventually Shade stopped and looked around. She didn't recognize anything in this part of the woods. She, like most Pleasant Hollow sprites, rarely left the village, and when she did, rarely went far. The village had everything the sprites needed to be content—nuts and berries to eat, water to drink, trees to live in, acorns to toss, etc.—and that was good enough for them. Pleasant Hollow sprites rarely felt the need to seek out anything outside the hollow.

Spying a comfortable-looking log, Shade took a seat and had a think. She looked up at the red and gold leaves and the purple clouds floating in the orange sky. It would be night soon. *Now what do I do?* She wondered. *I have no food, no water, no clothes except the ones on my back, no bed to sleep in—nothing except this book in my hands.*

Shade looked back and realized that if she flew, she could probably make it back to Pleasant Hollow before nightfall. Sure, she had no house to go back to, but someone would doubtless let her stay with them until they had built her a new tree house, which would probably only take them a few days. *But why?* she wondered. *Why go back to a place full of dimwits who've never liked me? No, I'll never go back.*

Shade resolutely nodded her head. She was certain. And then she was uncertain. *If I don't go home,* she wondered, *then where do I go?* She put her hands over her eyes and groaned, "Oh, where the dingle-dangle am I going?"

"That is an excellent question," she heard a voice squeak, "and one that I might be able to help with."

Shade uncovered her eyes to find a tiny little man with the eyes and wings of a fly who glowed like a firefly smiling at her. Now, when I say "tiny," I do mean tiny. While your average sprite—like most small varieties of fairies, such as pixies and brown-ies—is from head to toe about the size of one of your cats if he stood on his hind legs—let's say your tabby, Major Tom, since your calico, Mr. Wellington, is still a kitten—this fellow was no bigger than the tip of a sprite's pinky. In his hand, he held a lantern three times his size that shone with brilliant white light.

"You can, eh?" Shade asked, an eyebrow cocked with suspicion.

"Oh, yes," the little fellow said as he buzzed in a figure-eight pattern. "I know these woods inside and out! Just tell me where you're headed, and I'll make sure you get there."

"Like fun you will! You're a Will o' the Wisp!" Shade pointed an accusatory finger at him.

"What? No! I'm not—" the wisp began, but Shade

shushed him, opened her book, and jabbed a page near the back with her finger.

"Right here," she declared. "And I quote: 'The Will o' the Wisp is a very small variety of imp found in woods and swamps who uses its lamp to trick travelers into losing their way, often to a bloody demise.'"

"Well, that's very true of Will o' the Wisps," the tiny man agreed, nodding his head. "But I'm an Anthony o' the Wisp. I do the opposite of Will o' the Wisps and help travelers find their way as safely as possible."

Shade frowned and held the page of Radishbottom's book up for him to see. "You look just like the drawing of a Will o' the Wisp."

Anthony o' the Wisp looked down and cleared his throat. "Well, um, that's because I was born a Will o' the Wisp . . . but I changed my name to Anthony. I'd rather not be associated with Will o' the Wisps. Or they'd rather not be associated with me, as the case may be."

Shade's frown softened. "Why not?"

"Because I want to help travelers, not trick them," he said, giving her a little smile. "Since I know these woods so well, it's easy for me to help people find places in it. It's lots more work to get them lost or hurt. Why work so hard to be mean when it's so much easier to be nice?"

It was a question that Shade had often wondered herself.

"So where do you want to go?" Anthony asked.

Home, Shade thought sadly. *Home with my mother and father.* She looked down at the book in her lap and wiped a tear from her eye. *Home with Mom and Dad and all of our lovely books. But they're all gone now. But . . .* Shades eyes widened. "Books," she said. "Someplace with books. Lots of books. Maybe even . . . a library? I've read about them, and my father said there used to be a few, but he thought they were probably all gone now."

"Libraries?" Anthony's forehead wrinkled. "Never heard of them. And there aren't many readers in this forest that I've heard of . . . I could take you to the edge of the forest. There must be someplace out there that has books."

Shade shrugged. "Sounds like as good of a plan as any. If I decide to follow you."

"Well," Anthony said, "it seems to me that if you don't know where you're going, then I can't really get you lost, so you have nothing to lose in following me. This way!"

Anthony buzzed off into the trees as Shade got up and began walking after him. Anthony buzzed back after a moment. "Aren't you going to fly?"

"I don't fly." Shade crossed her arms.

Anthony smiled. "Then I suppose I'll just have to fly slower so you can keep up."

In which Shade meets a
Gentletroll of Refinement and
receives an invitation to tea . . .

That night, Shade slept in a clearing next to a cozy fire that Anthony made for her, her gray, black, white, and brown wings wrapped about her for warmth. When fully extended, her wings looked rather like the face of a ferocious owl about to attack— and owls occasionally did attack sprites foolish enough to be out at night. When they hung lax, they appeared rather drab. Neither look had been terribly popular back in Pleasant Hollow. In fact, she had often been teased about them when she was little.

When she awoke the next morning, Anthony presented her with a brown leather backpack that nicely coordinated with her brown skin and her tan silk tunic—the bright colors most sprites dyed their clothes didn't fit her more modest tastes. "Here," he said as he dragged it to her. "It's a bit big, but that might help you fit it around your wings. I filled it with nuts and berries for your journey to wherever you may be going. And there's also a notebook, pen, and ink in there. Maybe you can make a note about Anthony o' the Wisps and anything else you find that's not in your book."

"Thanks," Shade said as she inspected the backpack. "Where did you get it, and what's this reddish-brown stain?"

Anthony's glowing skin, already quite pale, grew even paler. "Let's just say that what your book said about Will o' the Wisps answers both of those questions and not go into any gruesome details, shall we?"

"Let's," Shade agreed as she put Radishbottom's book into the bag and fitted it around her wings, trying to touch the stains as little as possible. Once she had it on, she extended her wings and gave them a couple short flaps.

Shade walked briskly behind Anthony as he led her to the forest's edge. Anthony stopped and landed on a sizable stump and pointed through the trees. "I can't say for certain since I've never left the forest, but I believe there's a town in that direction. I've also heard rumors of a vicious troll who preys on travelers somewhere hereabouts. Even if there isn't one, do be careful. I've heard things are more dangerous out there since the last war."

Shade had heard similar things here and there from the rare travelers passing through Pleasant Hollow over the years. Apparently the war her mother had fought in, the latest between the Seelie Court (the good fairies who had ruled for centuries) and the Sluagh Horde (the evil fairies who had tried to overthrow them for just as long), had ended in an uneasy truce brokered after the deaths of the rulers of both sides. The new Seelie king, Julius, and the new ruler of the Sluagh, Queen Modthryth, had agreed to an ill-defined joint dominion over Elfame, the realm of the fairies, with the result being that people were so unclear as to what laws were in effect where that, essentially, there were no laws or clear authority in most places. Aside from Shade and her father, the sprites of Pleasant Hollow, being mostly isolated from the rest of the world, had little interest in who won the war and what laws might exist outside the village.

"I'll be as safe as I can," she assured Anthony. Shade was about to leave when she looked back at the little man. She stopped, bit her lip, and glanced out past the trees then back at Anthony. Since her father's death, she had preferred to be alone, but the little wisp had been so kind. Plus, truth be told, she was nervous about leaving the Merry Forest for the first time. "Want to come along?" she asked anxiously.

Anthony smiled, and his multifaceted eyes glinted up at her then gazed out at the wide-open, grassy plains just past the forest. His smile vanished, and he began wringing his hands. "Um, I'd love to, but . . . I can't . . ."

"Oh, right!" Shade said. "Radishbottom says that wisps are magically bound to the forests and bogs they're born in. You can't leave, can you?"

"Uh, that's not exactly . . ." Anthony scratched his head and cleared his throat. "Actually, we're not magically bound or anything. We're just . . . terrified of open spaces. Terrified."

"Really? Have you—"

"*Terrified!*"

In the unlikely event that you've ever seen a fly cry, you'll know that when they do all the little mirrored squares that make up their eyes steam up until beads of water form and run down in streaks, just like the mirror in your bathroom when you are forced (and I agree with you, most unfairly) to take a long, hot bath after a good play. That's exactly what happened with Anthony. Shade felt horrible as tears ran down his eyes to sizzle on the skin of his cheeks—for the glowing makes them rather hot, you understand. "Oh, I . . .

I'm sorry," Shade muttered, not being used to apologizing for the things she did and said. "I didn't mean . . . I just . . . I liked spending time with you and thought maybe . . ."

"You did?" Anthony asked, fishing a handkerchief out of a pocket and polishing his eyes. "That's very nice. I wish I could but . . ."

"No, I understand. Thank you so much for everything," Shade said and began to walk away from the woods where she had spent her entire life.

Now, when I mentioned grassy plains before, you probably pictured something like the lawn in your yard, which is usually kept well trimmed by your parents or, when it gets too hot for them, by either you or your older brother (who really shouldn't use that kind of language while he does it). That's not what wild grasses look like, however. Yes, some grow low, but many of them grow tall and lush and weedy, which is exactly what Shade laboriously pushed and tromped through, using language that would make even your brother blush as she did so.

In time, she was so hot and sweaty and frustrated that she was almost tempted to take to the air and fly. But she didn't. Memories of being called "fat acorn with wings" and other insulting names kept her grounded, so she pressed on miserably through the plains as the winds picked up and the skies darkened.

Eventually Shade found herself on the edge of a wide river whose waters rushed past. Thirsty from her journey, Shade made her way down the rocky banks to the water's edge and drank from her cupped hands, getting quite wet in the mist from the waters crashing against stone. Pushing back the dripping black ringlets of hair that hung down her forehead, Shade gazed to the far shore. With those winds blowing, she knew she wouldn't be able to fly across, so she walked along the riverbank, hoping to find a place where the river would be narrow enough to fly across.

In time, however, she spied a bridge—an oak one with stone foundations at both ends and sturdy supports anchored deep in the riverbed. Shade quickened her pace, eager to cross. But when she made it to the bridge, she found the end of it blocked by a long length of chain in the middle of which hung a wooden sign that stated in lovely red calligraphy:

Troll Bridge
Cross at your own peril.

What's more, just to the side of the bridge was a large wooden chair with a red and white striped umbrella open above it. Propped against the chair was another sign painted in the same delicate hand as the other:

Troll is currently on break.
Please menace yourself in the meantime.

Sincerely,
The Management

Being such an exceptionally well-read little sprite, Shade was quite knowledgeable about trolls, as I'm sure you are as well. For example, she, like you, was well aware that trolls stand between six and eight feet tall and have wild manes of coarse black hair running from the tops of their foreheads all the way down to their tail-bones, pointy wolfish ears, rough green-gray skin, little piggy eyes, long boar-like tusks jutting up from their lower jaws, and arms so long that their sharp-taloned hands often drag along the ground as they walk. What's more, Shade knew, as I'm sure you do, that bridge trolls are the wiliest variety of troll, so she naturally thought the sign on the chair had the makings of a trap.

Just a little way down a dirt path that led to the bridge stood what to Shade was an immense, palatial home, but what we, not being little sprites who have never left their forest home, would consider a modest stone cottage, surrounded by well-tended garden beds filled with red, orange, and yellow snapdragons. *Anyone who lives this close to a troll bridge*, Shade concluded, *must know how to handle the beast. Maybe she can tell me how to trick it into letting me across or, better yet, how to defeat it once and for all and thus save the lives of other innocent travelers, just like in* The Chivalrous Tales of Sir Percy Dovetonsils *or* Ripping Yarns and Tales of Dashing-Do*!*

And so Shade hurried to the cottage door and was about to knock when she thought, *Wait! If the owner lives this close to the troll bridge, maybe she's in league with the monster.* Deciding to proceed with caution, Shade tiptoed around to the back and flitted up high enough to peek in windows. In the front of the cottage she spied a cozy living room filled with elegant chairs and a couch arranged around a fireplace whose mantel was covered with little knickknacks. Next was a small-to-us-large-to-her bedroom appointed with a quilt-covered bed, lace-doily-covered nightstands, and an ornate wooden armoire.

Given the finery that she saw, Shade was almost convinced that it belonged to either some exiled human noble or perhaps an elf-lord deposed from the Seelie Court (like Sir Elbederth the Blameless in Abalath's *Songs of Seelie and Sluagh*) until she came to the back and looked through the window into a tidy little kitchen. Seated at a table covered with a spotless white linen table cloth, sipping with raised pinky from an elegant china teacup, was a troll. And he was looking right at her.

Now at this point, good Reader, I would love to give you a nice gruesome description of a classic troll and share with you the horrible, bloody rage he flew into as he attacked our plucky little heroine, but, alas, I must again disappoint you. While it is true that the troll had appropriately green-gray skin and tusks, aside from that he didn't look terribly intimidating at all, what with his neatly coiffed hair pulled back into a mauve-ribboned ponytail, pince-nez spectacles perched on his pointy nose, and the purple velvet jacket and ivory waistcoat he wore over his frilly white shirt. Even the talons of his fingers were filed down and perfectly manicured. What's more, all he did upon seeing Shade was spit out his tea in surprise, sigh, stand up (revealing his tight, knee-length ivory pants, white stockings, and black, gold-buckled shoes), and come to the window. As he opened it, Shade took several steps back, having read about the length and snatching abilities of trolls' arms.

"Did you sneak across that bridge?" the troll asked wearily.

"No." Shade answered, leery of a trap.

"Well, thank goodness for that," the troll sighed. "See that you don't or I'll . . . do something quite nasty to you. With my claws and teeth and such. I am a bridge troll, you know." The troll looked thoughtful for a moment, nodded, muttered to himself, "Yes, I believe that will do," and shut the window.

Shade scratched her head. She knew that she had just been threatened, but she didn't *feel* threatened. Deciding to test things, she walked over to the bridge, removed the chain, and crossed to the other side, where she found three black goats grazing in the field beyond. Noting with some interest that they were quite large for goats and that all three had puffball tails and extra-long ears, Shade walked back across the bridge and tapped on the kitchen window.

The troll put down his teacup and opened the window. "Yes?" he asked, frowning.

Shade pointed over her shoulder. "Did you know that I just crossed your bridge? Twice?"

The troll shook his head. "Well, don't make it a third time then. I swear, yesterday it was that insufferable brownie and his pixie friend, and now you. It's getting so that a gentletroll of refinement can't sit down to afternoon tea without—"

"What if I do make it a third time?" Shade asked, crossing her arms. "What then?"

"I believe I previously established that it would be something quite nasty."

"No, it wouldn't."

"Now see here, my good sprite," the troll objected, pointing a long, bony, well-manicured finger at her. "If I say I'll do something nasty—"

"Then you're lying," Shade interrupted. "Those nails aren't sharp enough to cut butter, plus anything nasty you could do would soil those lovely clothes you're wearing. If it weren't for you being a troll, I'd say that you're a better fit for a garden party in Jayne Owlslyn's *Pride and Pixies* than for guarding a bridge."

The troll's eyes grew wide and he put a hand to his chest. "You've read *Pride and Pixies*?"

"Several times."

The troll grinned. "And you think that I— Well, let's not be so uncivilized as to talk Owlslyn through a window! Come around to the front and join me for tea, if you please."

The troll hurried off. Shade wondered briefly whether or not it was such a good idea to sit down to tea with a troll, but then headed to the front of the cottage to accept the troll's invitation, concluding that she, like the heroes and heroines of many of her favorite stories, would be clever enough to save herself if things took an unpleasant turn.

In which a lovely tea is interrupted by a pack of pugnacious púcas . . .

The troll ushered Shade in with a little bow. "Welcome to the humble abode of Chauncey X. Troggswollop, Esquire, Miss . . ."

"Shade," Shade replied as she headed toward the kitchen.

"Shade?" Chauncey asked as he followed her back. He poured tea in the smallest cup he had, which was still immense for her, since she was less than a third of his size. "I thought sprites had more . . . fanciful names than that. Full of descriptors and nature and whatnot."

"And I thought trolls lived under bridges and in caves."

Chauncey made a face. "Most do, but as a gentletroll of refinement, I absolutely refuse. Why, these clothes—custom-made by Tinkleton of Durrellbury—would be ruined by the muck and mire, and I'm liable to catch an ague from the damp. What's more—Oh, dear, pardon my manners! I can't expect you to *stand* for tea!"

Chauncey rushed out and returned with a stack of books of etiquette that he placed on one of the chairs. Shade climbed on top of them as Chauncey took a seat across from her and served her a slice of lemon cake.

"Isn't living under bridges and eating travelers the whole point of being a troll?" she asked before lifting the teacup with both her hands and taking a sip.

"No, living under bridges and eating people may be common—and disgusting—practice, but neither is the *point* of being a bridge troll," Chauncey said civilly, taking a sip of his own tea. "The point of being a bridge troll is to protect and preserve one's bridge. We bridge trolls are born as soon as someone gets the idea to build a bridge somewhere. Once it's completed, we find our way to it and defend it until either we die or the bridge is destroyed."

Shade considered this as she nibbled at her lemon cake, which was moist and delicious. "What happens if the bridge gets destroyed?"

A dreamy look came over Chauncey's face. "Then we're free to leave. Travel the world. Attend garden parties and royal levees. Oh, I rather wish that dratted thing out there would burn to the ground!"

"Why not just leave?" Shade asked. "You're clearly not happy out here."

"If only I could . . ." Chauncey sighed. "But I'm magically bound to see to it that the bridge is defended. So I'm stuck here out in the country, with only the occasional visit from my uncle, my books of etiquette and Owlslyn, and now a lovely spot of tea with a fellow admirer of the darling Ms. Owlslyn to make life bearable."

Feeling sorry for the troll, Shade didn't have the heart to tell him that she didn't much care for *Pride and Pixies*. "But surely such a pleasant and refined gentletroll as yourself has made friends amongst your neighbors?" she said.

"Neighbors?" Chauncey scoffed. "What neighbors?"

"I saw three púcas on the other side of the bridge. Don't they—"

"Púcas!" Chauncey rushed to the window, sloshing tea about. "Three of them you say? Sweet Saint Figgymigg!"

Shade followed him. "What's the problem? I've read about púcas. They're harmless tricksters, right?"

"Not these púcas," Chauncey replied grimly.

Shade looked out the window to see that the púcas had changed shape. I'm sure that you know all about púcas, being as well-versed in fairy lore as you no doubt are, so I won't insult your intelligence by explaining that púcas are black-furred shapechangers who can take the shape of goats, rabbits, ponies, or people but not completely, thus making them look like goats with rabbit tails, ponies with bunny ears, rabbits with goat horns, and so forth. I will let you know, however, that in this case the three púcas had taken the shape of little men with the tails and hooves of ponies, the noses and teeth of rabbits, and the horns and beards of goats (púcas are especially bad at mimicking human form). As Shade watched, the púcas kicked at the railings, stomped on the planks of the bridge, and made rude gestures at the cottage.

"Oi! Come on out, ye great foul troll and get what's comin' to ye!" the largest of the púcas shouted, rolling his Rs and elongating his Os as he did so. He followed up his challenge by breaking part of a railing with a fierce kick.

"What's gotten into them?" Shade asked. "Nothing I've ever read has suggested that púcas could be so—"

"Rude? Violent? Have such horrible fashion sense?" Chauncey asked as he dabbed at the sweat forming on his forehead with a lace handkerchief. "Well, my dear Miss Shade, I would wager that there are a good many things out in the world—like bookish sprites, gentletrolls, and murderous púcas—that you have never read anything about. Now if you will excuse me, I must go tend to this."

"Wait!" Shade grabbed his arm. "You can't go out there! They could kill you!"

Chauncey sighed. "They very likely will. According to my uncle, they've killed a good number of bridge trolls already, and I'm likely to be the next. But I must go defend my bridge."

"Why? You hate the thing! You said so yourself."

Chauncey opened the door. "Love it or hate it, it's my bridge, and it is my duty to defend it. I'm sorry that our time together was so brief, Miss Shade. I advise you to stay in here and spare yourself the unpleasantness that is to follow. If I do not return, please feel free to take as many Owlslyn and etiquette books, lemon cakes, and cucumber sandwiches as you like.

In spite of Shade's protests, Chauncey marched out the door and over to the bridge with Shade right on his heels. As he drew near, the púcas paused in their wanton assault on the bridge. The biggest one pointed at

Chauncey. "Oo la la! Jaimie, Jimmie, take a look at the great jessie we got here!"

"He's dressed right bonnie, he is, Jock!" the middle-sized one laughed.

"Too bad he's got a face like a skelped erse," the smallest one bleated.

"I would rather be a 'jessie' with a face like a 'skelped erse'—whatever that means—than an ill-mannered hooligan like the three of you," Chauncey said coolly. He started to take off his velvet jacket. "Now, if you'll just allow me a moment to remove this lovely garment—it's a Tinkleton of Durrellbury, you know— then we can—Oof!"

Before Chauncey could finish, Jock, the biggest of the púcas, charged and butted him in the side with his horns. Chauncey staggered, the seam at the top of his coat sleeve tearing as he did so.

Chauncey took off his pince nez and looked at the tear, his eyes widening and face darkening. "How dare you, sir!" he roared and swatted Jock with the back of his hand, sending him flying.

Seeing their brother struck down, the other two leapt into action. Jimmie, the littlest, butted the back of Chauncey's knees with his horns as Jaimie, the middle-sized one, jumped and kicked him in the chest with his hooves. Chauncey toppled, flailing, into the dirt. "My lovely clothes!" he cried as the three púcas fell upon him, pummeling him with clenched fists and hooves.

Shade was beside herself. She ran around the four brawling figures, shouting at them to stop. The púcas and troll didn't react in the least to her cries, but what more could a little sprite do? Just as she thought all was lost, Chauncey staggered to his feet, swinging his great troll hands wildly as the three púcas hung onto him, punching and kicking and biting him all over. Seeing that Chauncey was perilously close to the edge of the riverbank, Shade dug her little feet in the dirt and sprinted at him. With a leap of her legs and a flap of her wings, she flew up and hit him in the small of the back and sent all five of them—troll, sprite, and púcas three—tumbling down the bank and into the river.

Chauncey and the púcas splashed about crying,

"Oh my!" "Ach, no!" and words so dreadful that you might get your mouth washed out with soap just for thinking them. Louder than all of them, however, was Shade. "All right, you dingle-dangle dunces! Knock it off, or your lives won't be worth a red hot donkle, you stupid thistlepricks!"

Shade knew that any one of those creatures could crush a two-foot-tall sprite without batting a púcaish or trollish eye, but she was wet and mad and didn't care. The biggest of the púcas gave an impressed whistle. "Awfully foul geggy for a wee lass, init? Ye kiss yer mother with that mouth?"

Shade pointed her finger menacingly in the púca's face, who twitched nervously. "You! Jack!"

"Jock."

"Whatever! Why are you and the nitwit twins attacking Chauncey?"

"We're not twins," the littlest one objected. "Jaimie's clearly bigger than—"

"Shut it!" Shade growled, pointing at Jimmie, who dutifully shut it. "Why?"

"He's a troll!" Jock declared. "Just like the one who killed Angus, our dear seventh cousin four times removed!"

"We've vowed to get bloody vengeance on all the evil trolls of the world and make it safe for poor little púcas who just want to cross bridges to get to greener pastures everywhere," Jaimie added, tearing up.

"Evil, dirty, hackit, savage trolls!" Jimmie spat. "Livin' under bridges, snatchin' and eatin' poor folk!"

Shade crossed her arms. "Does Chauncey here look 'dirty,' 'savage,' or . . . whatever else you called him? Does he even look like he lives under a bridge?"

The four turned to look at Chauncey, who was daintily dabbing at mud on his waistcoat with a lace handkerchief. "This whole Tinkleton ensemble—ruined! Oh, you may as well butt me to death, you brutes!" he moaned, flinging the handkerchief into the river. "Life lived without finery is simply not worth living!"

Jock cocked an eyebrow. "All right, ye may have a point. But we still probably saved you from—"

"A delightful tea and pleasant conversation!" Shade interrupted.

Chauncey brightened a bit at that. "How very sweet of you to say, my dear!

"Ye two were havin' tea?" Jimmie asked.

"Yes," they answered in unison.

"And ye weren't fixin' to eat her?" Jaimie asked.

Chauncey made a face. "Absolutely not! Eating one's guests—the idea! What a horrible breach of etiquette! Besides, I never eat meat. Terrible for the figure, plus . . ."

"Gives ye wind, does it?" Jimmie chuckled. Chauncey's lips pursed as he gave a slight nod.

"Satisfied?" Shade asked, glaring at the púcas.

Jock, Jaime, and Jimmie exchanged glances, then shrugged their shoulders.

"Well, if I'm not to be murdered," Chauncey declared. "Would all of you like a spot of tea while I change into something else before I die of shame?"

In which boxes and bags prove
surprisingly important and interesting . . .

S hade scribbled notes about púcas, gentletrolls,
and Anthonys o' the Wisp in her notebook
while Chauncey changed into equally elegant
new clothes and the púcas devoured the tea cakes,
cookies and sandwiches. "In our defense," Jock said as
he munched his tenth cucumber sandwich, "ye are a
troll."

"And ye've scared a lot of folk 'round aboot," Jaimie added.

"Exactly how I don't ken," Jimmie muttered, eyeing Chauncey's velvet jacket.

Chauncey sighed. "I know. It's tiresome, having to terrify everyone who comes by, but I must defend my bridge. The more a bridge is used, the more it falls apart."

Shade looked up from her notebook. "Wait. So you just have to make sure the bridge lasts? You aren't fighting to defend your territory?"

Chauncey waved his hand dismissively. "Dance a jig on it, for all I care, if you can guarantee it won't do the dratted thing any harm. Speaking of which, you púcas have left my bridge rather the worse for wear."

"And we'll be happy to fix it up before we go," Jock said.

"Well, not happy," Jaimie corrected.

"A wee bit grumbly while we do it, to be honest with ye," Jimmie added. "But we'll do it."

An idea began to form in Shade's mind. "Are púcas good at woodworking?"

"Not in the main, but we three are," Jaimie replied.

"Could you make something like this?" Shade asked as she sketched a box with a hinged lid with a small slot in the middle.

The púcas looked at it and nodded. "Aye, we could do that," Jock said, stroking his little beard. "Why?"

"Well, I just remembered a story from *Le Warte d'Arty* about a knight who demanded all of a traveler's money whenever one crossed his bridge—"

"Oh, heavens," Chauncey gasped, placing a hand on his chest. "You're not suggesting that I become a . . . a common highwayman!"

Jock frowned as well. "That might be a wee bit better than eatin' folk, but doin' it if they can't pay—"

"I've told you, I never eat—"

"*No*," Shade said firmly. "Nobody eats anyone. We put these boxes at each end of the bridge with a little sign asking for donations in exchange for use of the bridge.

"Won't most use it without payin'?" Jaimie asked.

"I would," Jimmie said.

"Not if they know a troll defends the bridge," Shade answered.

"It's true—I can be quite intimidating," Chauncey said, lifting his pinky and daintily sipping his tea.

"And then you use the money to pay for bridge maintenance," Shade said, crossing her arms and leaning back in her seat.

"A troll toll bridge!" Chauncey clapped his hands. "Oh, it is a fabulous idea!"

With tea finished, the púcas began repairing the bridge and making the toll boxes while Chauncey quizzed Shade about her favorite parts of *Pride and Pixies* and whether she liked Elzesplat Bunting or Mr. Doosey better ("The correct answer, my dear," he declared, "is *both!*") before preparing a lovely six-course meal for the five.

Over dinner, Shade's situation was discussed. Chauncey, having found her delightful company, offered her the chance to live with him. When she declined (while books of etiquette and Jayne Owlslyn were better than no books at all, they were still far from satisfying), it was decided that one of the púcas would give her a ride the next day to the nearest fairy town. The other púcas would remain to continue the repairs and resent the third for taking off on a pleasant day's ride.

At bedtime, Chauncey showed Shade to his spare bedroom. The room was smaller than all the rest, but it contained a comfy little bed (little to us, again, but enormous to Shade), a polished maple dresser, and watercolor landscapes on the walls. It would have been wonderfully cozy if the room weren't crammed full of suitcases and steamer trunks.

"You must pardon the mess, I'm afraid," Chauncey said as he cleared a path to the bed. "My house is rather small, and my vacations take up quite a bit of space."

"Vacations?" Shade said, looking at all the suitcases. "I thought you said that you never get the chance to leave the bridge."

"I don't. My dear uncle is the traveler, but he's nice enough to bring me his vacations when he's done with them. Would you like to see?"

Shade shrugged. "Sure."

Chauncey considered several trunks and bags before fwumping a large tan suitcase on the bed. "Oh, this is a lovely one!"

Chauncey snapped open the suitcase, and Shade peered in, expecting souvenirs, much like the shells or wooden figurines or tiny empty bottles that smell like juice that's gone bad that your Aunt Gwen always brings you after one of her vacations. What Shade saw instead was a pebble beach with the sun shining cheerily in a cloudless azure sky while waves lapped gently along the shore. Shade gaped in amazement. "What— How—?"

"Lovely isn't it? Let's have a little walk," Chauncey said, taking Shade by the hand and giving a little jump. Before she knew what was happening, Shade could smell salty sea air and feel the sun warming her back and water tickling her toes.

"How can you have a place in a box?" Shade asked as she bent down and picked up a shell, turning it in her hands, trying to decide if it and everything else was real.

Chauncey closed his eyes, took in a deep breath, and exhaled contentedly. "When my uncle's done with one of his vacations, he packs it up and brings it to me to enjoy since he knows I can't go off and have one myself."

Shade shook her head. "That makes no sense."

Chauncey picked up a stone and skipped it across the water. "Actually, it's exceptionally sensible. Most people take all sorts of nonsense they don't really need when they go off on vacation and then, when it's over, they pack it all up plus useless little knickknacks and gewgaws that they pick up as souvenirs and bring it all home. Uncle Lesley, when he's done with a vacation, packs that up instead and brings it to me so that I can enjoy it, although I do believe he keeps the best ones for himself. Makes much more sense than bringing home a bunch of rubbish, if you ask me." Chauncey clasped his hands behind his back and strolled along the beach, turning his face up to the sun.

"But that doesn't . . . I mean, that's not a real . . . Wait!" Shade called after him.

After a baffling but otherwise terribly pleasant hour by the sea, Chauncey and Shade climbed back out of the suitcase, went outside to wish the púcas a good night (Chauncey had offered them the chance to sleep in his living room, but they passed, declaring sleeping in a house to be "a bit too posh" for them), and then settled in for the night.

The next morning it was decided that Jimmie would take the form of a pony—with goat horns and a rabbit tail—and give Shade a ride to the town of Gypsum-upon-Swathmud, which was about a day's ride away. Just before they left, Chauncey, dabbing at his eyes with a handkerchief, brought her her backpack

"I've filled your bag with goodies for the road— don't worry though, I made sure that nothing will get on your books. And I wanted to give you a little token of my thanks, my esteem, and my undying affection." Chauncey turned the bag to reveal that he had strapped a small, thin briefcase to its front. "It was a short but beautiful little vacation and I want you to have it. You never know when you'll need to get away from things for a while."

The troll wished her well and gave her a kiss on each cheek.

"Do that to me, ye great big ponce, and you'll get a clype from me hoof," Jimmie grumbled.

"Don't mind him," Jock said, putting a hand on Chauncey's shoulder. "He's all bum and parsley, he is."

"Safe travels, lassie," Jaimie called after Shade as she rode off on the back of the galloping púca-pony. She smiled with satisfaction as they sped across a bridge and past a pair of wooden boxes with slits in their tops. Above each box was a sign on which was written in large, elegant letters:

Troll Toll Bridge
Please consider leaving a generous donation as you pass to pay for maintenance and better guarantee the safety and well-being of yourself and all travelers.

Sincerely,
Chauncey X. Troggswollop, Esq.
Bridge Custodian and Gentletroll of Refinement

6

In which Shade experiences business as usual at the Crooked Rook . . .

"Looks like yer in luck, lass," Jimmie declared as he galloped toward Gypsum-upon-Swathmud in the light of the setting sun. He jerked his horned pony head at the carts and wagons driving into and out of the village and the scores of fairy folk milling about the stone and thatched-roof buildings there. "The goblin market's right hoachin' and runs all day and all night. If there's books aboot, they'll either be here or somebody here will know where to find 'em."

The púca stopped just outside of the town, and Shade hopped down. "Do you really want to head back tonight?" Shade asked. She was nervous to be on her own there in that new, bustling place. "I'm sure whatever inn I stay at will have a stable for you to sleep in."

Jimmie shook his head. "No. Never have liked towns. Too dirty and too full of eejits dumb enough to live in 'em."

Shade said goodbye and watched Jimmie ride into the twilight before turning to face the village. Surveying the immense buildings all crowded together and watching all manner of fairy folk—rich and poor, big and small, pudgy and thin, beautiful and hideous—as they came and went and milled about, listening to the hawkers' calls and merchants' haggling and every sort of laugh and scream and chatter imaginable, Shade was both excited and terrified. Gypsum-upon-Swathmud was so much more . . . well, just so much more *everything* than Pleasant Hollow.

Resolved, Shade marched toward the town. Right on its edge, she spied a run-down inn with a cracked, graying old sign hanging askew above its door, one end noticeably higher than the other, with the words "The Crooked Rook" above a painting of a black bird wearing an eye patch. It didn't look (or smell) like a good place to eat or sleep, but it reminded Shade of something straight from the pages of a favorite book of hers, Carolus the Stripling's *Meager Expectations*, so staying there had the sort of immense romantic appeal that usually leads to incredibly terrible choices being made.

When Shade walked through the swinging doors into the Crooked Rook's tavern, her eyes immediately began to water at the oniony, turnipy smell billowing from a large bubbling stew pot that wrestled for dominance with the stench of pipe and cigar smoke. Fairies of all sorts—goblins, hobgoblins, pixies, brownies, kobolds, dwarves, knockers, elves, a couple cats wearing hats and boots, and many others—sat in dim lantern light on rickety seats around battered tables or stood by the fire, drinking strong-smelling things out of scabby leather mugs. The scars that most of them sported and the foul language they used (almost immediately upon entering, Shade heard every rude word she had ever known plus seven more) made Shade uneasy, but she remembered one of Radishbottom's travel tips: "When entering an unfamiliar tavern, always act completely at ease, and when staying at an unfamiliar inn, always haggle over the price of a room."

Shade squared her tiny shoulders, sneered slightly in an attempt to look tough, and sauntered to the bar. On her way, she passed a large table at which sat a bunch of rough, scary-looking fairies wearing red caps. They played cards with a brownie wearing a narrow-brimmed hat and a pixie with a headful of fluffy yellow curls that, combined with his thin frame and green clothes, made him look rather like a blond dandelion ready for its seeds to blow away. A battered green top-hat was perched on top of his puffball head. Shade did a double-take when she noticed that one of the red-capped players was a human, and an especially rough-looking one with a mashed nose, ears that looked like they had been chewed up and spat onto either side of his head, and a painful-looking scar that started high on his forehead and ran all the way down to his chin, a dirty-looking patch mercifully hiding his right eye.

While she had occasionally seen most types of fairies thanks to the odd traveler passing through Pleasant Hollow, she had never actually seen a human before. Everything she read had taught her that fairy dealings with humans were rare. For one thing, their immense size (bigger than any fairy except for trolls, ogres, and giants) and ability to handle iron (which causes intense pain to fairies) made them extremely dangerous. For another, humans can only see fairies at certain times (dawn, dusk, Halloween, The Feast of St. Figgymigg, etc.) or under special conditions (charming, abduction, having a fairy spit in their eyes, being the half-nephew of a cheesemaker, etc.). Based on his looks, Shade guessed that he had been abducted as a baby and raised by evil fairies to serve as a warrior or thug. When he looked up from his cards in her direction, she quickly looked down at her bare feet and hurried to the bar and climbed onto an empty stool.

When the goblin bartender eventually turned his black- and brown-furred, limp-eared Rottweiler head in Shade's direction (for, as you know, goblins are covered in fur and have animal-like heads), Shade sat up a little straighter and frowned, trying to look like a sprite not to be trifled with. The goblin rolled his eyes. "What'll it be, miss?" he grumbled.

"I'd like a room for the night."

The bartender spat in the glass in his hand and started polishing it. "Two silver."

"I'll give you one," Shade said resolutely.

The bartender plunked the glass down on the bar. "Oh, hagglin' are we? Fine. Three silver: two for the room, one for insultin' the Crooked Rook by saying it ain't worth two silver."

"What?" Shade asked. "No. You're supposed to . . ."

"And now it's four silver. I'm tackin' one on for continuin' to waste my time."

"But, but—"

"And another for the rude language."

"I didn't mean that kind of bu—"

""'Ey, why you pick-a on the little country sproot?" the brownie from the card game asked in a thick, musical accent filled with extra vowel sounds and trilled Rs. Like all brownies, this one had shiny golden skin like polished wood and dark brown hair poking out from every edge of the too small hat that sat on the back of his head. In fact, all of his chocolate brown clothes—jacket, vest, shirt, pants—seemed a size or two too small. The brownie leaned on the bar and gave Shade a wink. "If Snarlful don't give-a you the house rate, I give-a you the directions to the Dirty Jerkin or the Boar's Backside or—"

"All right," the goblin bartender interrupted. "Two silver . . . *if* I've got a vacancy. Now what do you want, Ginch?"

"A couple more drinks for me and my partner," the brownie said.

"Four copper."

"Put-a it on my tab."

"Cash in advance," Snarlful half-snarled, putting his hands on his hips.

The brownie raised a finger. "How's about I—"

"Cash," Snarlful fully snarled. "In advance."

"All right, all right!" The brownie slapped a silver coin on the bar.

The goblin snatched up the coin and filled the glass he had just spit-polished with amber liquid. "I'll put the change toward what you and the pixie owe."

"Fatcha-coota-matchca, gooblins!" the brownie cried, taking his drinks and heading back to the card game.

"As for you," Snarlful said to Shade. "Two silver for a room. In advance."

"Fine," Shade muttered and put two silver coins from

the money that Chauncey had given her on the bar. They quickly vanished into the goblin's pocket.

"I'll let you know when it's ready," the bartender said. "Want a drink or some food while you wait?"

Shade looked over at the noxious, bubbly stew pot. "No."

The bartender shrugged and went off to take orders from a couple dwarves. Shade took a worn, uncomfortable seat by the fire, pulled out Radishbottom's book, and waited. And waited. And waited.

"When will my room be ready?" Shade demanded after reading and holding her nose to keep the stench of the place at bay for over an hour.

"Tomorrow night." The goblin chuckled, elbowing the rat-faced hobgoblin he had been talking to. "Probably."

"You cheat!" Shade yelled at the goblin, who, at four feet tall, towered over her. "Give me back my dingle-dangle money, you crook!"

Snarlful and his hobgoblin friend snickered. "Said 'in advance,' didn't I? Never said anything about tonight."

"All right, you shifty slug-licker! You'll be donkled four ways when I get the law on you!" Shade shouted as she stormed out of the bar as the bartender and his friend laughed heartily.

Shade marched down the dirt street in the torch-light, not sure where to go or what to do. She was in a strange place where she knew nobody, she had no place to stay and didn't know where else to go, and she had just been cheated and laughed at. She felt furious and humiliated and scared and miserable.

Ducking into a narrow alleyway, she leaned against the wall and tried to calm herself down. Just as she started to feel a little bit better, a window high above opened and dirty, smelly water splashed down, soaking her dress. After shouting things that I don't dare repeat (much to the relief of your parents), Shade kicked the side of the building hard, forgetting that stone walls always beat bare toes. As she hopped around on one foot, hands holding the injured one as she did so, she wondered what more could happen to her.

7

In which more happens to her . . .

The pain in Shade's foot subsided, and she began to calm down. *I'll find a place to stay first,* she decided. *What did that brownie say? The Jerkin? The Boar's something? I'll find one of those and get situated and—*

Her thoughts were interrupted by a cry of "In-a here!" followed by two small figures crashing into her, sending all three tumbling to the ground.

"Hey!" Shade cried as she disentangled herself from the other two. "Watch where you're going. You're—"

"'Ey! It's-a the little country sproot!" cried one of the two as he stood up and brushed off his too-tight brown suit. Suddenly he snapped his fingers. "Professor, you still got-a the sproot wings from the job we pull-a in Upper Swinetoe?"

The other figure sprang up on his two very long legs (which, in spite of the baggy pants, Shade could see bent the opposite way of her own, like the legs of a grasshopper) and nodded vigorously. His pale, pinkish-white skin and blond curls almost glowed in the moonlight as he rummaged deep in a pocket inside his oversized jacket before pulling out a battered and bent pair of fake butterfly wings that seemed far too big to fit in the pocket they had just come from. The brownie grabbed them and strapped them to his back. "That's-a fine! And the wig?"

The pixie reached back into his jacket and pulled out a shoulder-length red wig and plopped it on the brownie's head. "Okay, now you!" the brownie said.

The pixie made a frenzied search of the many pockets in his jacket and pants before shaking his head.

"You no got-a the other disguise?"

The pixie shook his head.

"Okay . . . you put-a you jacket over you head and look-a sad. You'll-a be the sick old granmama."

The pixie nodded then threw his jacket over his head and made a sad, sick face. It was very similar to the one you tried to use to stay home to avoid that spelling quiz that you forgot to study for, but the pixie's was much more convincing.

"Great! Now the three of us will—"

"What the dingle-dangle donkle is going on here?" Shade demanded.

The pixie opened his mouth wide and covered it with a hand and pointed at Shade with the other. "'Ey, you kiss-a you mother with that—" the brownie began.

"What's going on? And what do you mean 'the three of us'?"

"Well, it's-a like this," the brownie explained. "My

partner and I, we play-a the cards with those Sluagh red caps back at the Rook—"

"What's a 'red cap'?" Shade asked.

"What's-a the red cap?" The brownie looked at her incredulously. "Ha-ha! Boy, you really are-a the little country sproot! After the last war, a lotta the Sluagh run-a around in the red caps to look-a tough and let-a everybody know they the big, tough Sluagh. So like I say, we play-a with the red caps and there was-a the little misunderstanding and now they wanna kill us."

"What misunderstanding?"

"They think-a we cheat! I no know why. You know, Professor?"

The pixie shrugged and about twenty cards fell out of his sleeve, all of them the Ace of Hearts.

"He no know either. I think-a they just the sore losers. Anyway, you're-a gonna help us sneak away from 'em."

"And why would I do that?" Shade asked, crossing her arms.

"You wanna be responsible for somebody getting murdered?" the brownie asked.

"Of course not."

"Well, they gonna kill us if you no help," he replied before he and the pixie each grabbed one of her arms and started pulling her out of the alley with them.

"Wait! No! I never said I'd—Oof!"

Shade's objections were cut short as she bumped into the legs of the gigantic human she'd seen at the bar. He growled and put his hand on the handle of an immense knife strapped to his belt.

"Excuse me," Shade squeaked.

"Yeah, 'scuse her," the brownie said, pushing her gently back behind him. "She's-a the clumsy—always she's-a bumpin' and-a boompin' and-a—"

"What have we here?" asked a bat-faced hobgoblin who walked beside the human. He was soon joined by another hobgoblin, weasel-faced and equally hairless (but then, since I'm sure you know that hobgoblins look just like goblins but shorter and hairless, the "hairless" part really doesn't deserve any mention, does it?), and a short, leathery fairy with large feet and hands, spindly arms and legs from which its skin hung slack and wrinkled, crooked teeth, and rocks adorning his clothes. All of them wore dark red caps on their heads.

"Just the three country sproots come-a to the town for the market," the brownie said offhandedly.

"That so?" the hobgoblin asked, eyeing him closely. "Well, you look an awful lot like a cardsharpin' brownie we're lookin' for."

"I get-a that a lot. I just got-a one of those faces."

The hobgoblin pointed at the pixie, who frowned sadly. "And this looks an awful lot like his silent pixie partner."

"Well, that's-a my granmama. I get-a my face from her, so we look a lot alike other people."

The hobgoblin leaned forward and sniffed. "I think you two *are* the brownie and the pixie we're lookin' for."

The brownie waved his hand dismissively. "Aw, that's-a crazy! We're-a sproots! See-a the wings? Plus, you say-a the pixie, he no talk?"

"Yeah?"

"Hey, granmama, can-a you talk?"

The pixie nodded.

"See, she can-a talk, so she no can-a be the pixie!"

The leathery fairy, a spriggan, began to grow and swell, making the noise a balloon makes when it's being inflated, until finally it towered over even the human. It pointed a filthy, cracked fingernail at the pixie. "If that's a sproit, where's 'er wings, eh?"

"Yuh!" the human grunted. He drew his large, iron knife and held it close to the brownie's face. The brownie leaned away as if it were red-hot, which is exactly how it would have felt if the iron had touched him. "Whure?"

"Well . . uh . . . the thing is. . . eh . . ." the brownie stammered.

This whole time, Shade, terrified of the Sluagh goons, had considered telling the red-capped gang the truth about the situation to save herself, but said nothing for fear of what they might do to the brownie and the pixie, who seemed dishonest but harmless enough. Plus, she wasn't sure they would let her go even if she did give them the other two. Seeing the brownie finally at a loss for words, she leapt into action, crying her most convincing fake tears. "No, please don't hurt us!" she wailed. "Ever since mama was devoured by a screech owl and grandmama's wings were shredded by that badger, we've been ever so heartbroken. We thought that the goblin market would be a rare treat that might lift our woeful spirits, but now we're going to be killed because my father looks like some crooked, ugly brownie—"

"I no think-a anyone say he was-a ugly," the brownie said.

"He was," the hobgoblin replied.

"Yuh," agreed the human.

"—and because my poor, wingless grandmama looks like some smelly pixie!"

The pixie raised an arm, gave his armpit a sniff, and shrugged.

"I'd try to fly away," Shade continued, extending and giving her wings a half-hearted flap to show they were real, "but I'm sure I'd have no chance of escaping such fast, strong, and clever fairies—and human—as yourselves!"

"Darn roight we is!" the spriggan growled.

"Yuh," the human agreed.

"O woe is me! If only we could have been as quick and as lucky as that blabbermouthed brownie in the tight clothes and the mute pixie in the baggy green outfit who ran past just a little while ago!"

The fairies and human looked at each other. "Which way did they go?" the bat-faced hobgoblin barked.

Shade pointed past the Crooked Rook. "That way. Into the country where we just came from."

"Come on, boys!" the hobgoblin cried, waving his bronze sword in the air. "Let's get 'em!"

The rest, brandishing their weapons and shouting, ran off into the darkness of the country. The brownie laughed, and the pixie clapped his hands. "Ha-ha! That's-a the good one!" the brownie said, putting his arm around her shoulders. "You know, you're-a the pretty clever little sproot!"

"I know," Shade said, shrugging off his arm.

"I tell-a you what," the brownie declared. "You help-a us out, so now we help-a you out. We show-a you around the town, give-a you the hand—"

At that, the pixie reached into his pants pocket and pulled out a wooden hand that he held out to Shade.

"Not that kinda hand, partner," the brownie said. The pixie put it back in his pocket. "I'm-a Ginch—Rigoletto Ginch—and this is-a my partner, the Professor."

Shade arched an eyebrow at this. "He's a professor?"

"Well, he no talk, so I no know his name, so I call-a him the Professor. Doesn't he look-a like a professor?" Rigoletto Ginch asked.

Shade looked at the pixie. The pink tip of his tongue stuck out slightly from the goofy grin on his face. "No."

"Yeah, I no think-a so either," Ginch agreed. "So

like I say, you help-a us, so we take-a you under our wing."

The Professor pulled out the waistband of his pants, and a white bird fluttered into the air. He flapped his arms as it flew away, then pointed at Shade.

Shade looked from Ginch to the Professor and then back to Ginch. "I'll pass. I think you've gotten me into enough trouble already."

"But you no know how the gooblin market work," Ginch objected.

"I've read all about them. I know how they work," Shade said.

"Oh, you read-a the book so you the expert!" Ginch threw up his hands.

Shade turned her back on the two and walked toward the town center. "No, but I'm sure I know more than enough to take care of myself," she said with the exact sort of confidence that usually gets people into profoundly deep trouble.

8

In which Shade takes a trip to the
market, which may sound boring but
is much more eventful than the ones
your parents force you to go on . . .

Now, I'm sure that such a literate and worldly person as yourself, dear Reader, has at some point visited a place you read about in a book. When you did, no doubt you found that, regardless of how well the author described the place to you, it wasn't quite the same as what you pictured. For example, if you've ever visited Toad Hall, you may have found it a bit darker and smaller than you envisioned. Or perhaps the opposite was the case and, when visiting the mountains of Mordor, they were even bigger and more imposing than what you had expected.

Shade had the same experience as she walked into Gypsum-upon-Swathmud's town square and into her first goblin market. She found an unoccupied patch of wall on the edge of the market and took out Radishbottom's book. She found the section on goblin markets ("named thus for the exceptionally mercenary goblins that organize them and provide 'protection' for participating merchants" the book explained) and skipped to a part labeled "Tips for a Successful Visit," which read:

1. Prices for all goods are negotiable. Only a fool pays the asking price.
2. Everything has a price. Never take anything offered to you without first establishing what is expected in payment.

3. Thieves are known to prey on unwitting marketgoers. Be vigilant and, if possible, attend markets with at least one friend.

4. If you find yourself the victim of theft or another crime, raise a cry. If you are in luck, an officer of the Seelie Court may be present. If not, goblin-hired security will.

Shade closed the book and took a deep breath. *Okay,* she told herself. *You can do this! You've reformed a troll, stopped killer púcas, and tricked a goblin gang! Plus, you've read Radishbottom's book cover to cover many times, so you know how to handle a goblin market. All you have to do is go in there, look around, and . . . and then what? Puckernuts!*

Shade closed her eyes, moaned, and banged the back of her head against the wall behind her, hoping to knock some idea loose. Eventually she had one: *I'll look for someone who's selling books. If they have books, then maybe they'll know where more are. And maybe . . . maybe they'll have a copy of the book Mom and Dad gave me.* Shade's pulse raced at the thought. *If I can just find a copy of my book, then I'll know everything will be all right.*

Buoyed by the hope of regaining what she had lost as well as the assurance that comes from reading a book about whatever situation you are about to face, Shade plunged into the teeming hordes of the goblin market, scanning the carts and stalls for any sign of books. Everywhere she went, merchants tried as best they could to hock their wares.

"Finest of silks for the finest of sprites," an elegant elf said, holding out shimmering green cloth. "I'll give you a good price."

"No, thanks. I'll—ugh!" Shade reared back as a smelly fish was thrust under her nose.

"Fresh fish, I've got," declared the wolf-headed man holding it. "Und tasty rarebit. Maybe ve get you some voodchuck?"

"Yuck, no!" Shade said, backing away from the wulver and into a gnarled, wrinkled old trow with a cart filled with little glass bottles.

"Well, look at adorable little you," the old fairy cooed. "In the market for a love potion?"

"Absolutely not," Shade stated.

"Don't be so quick, dearie," the trow said, pinching Shade's cheeks. "With the extra puddin' you've got under the skin, you probably need—"

"To be left alone by crooks like you, Auntie Griselda. Push off!" A sprite with cobalt blue skin and white hair took Shade by the arm and steered her toward tables filled with jewelry set up in front of a covered wooden wagon with a door in its side. Shade gawped at the sprite, who looked like none she had ever seen before. It wasn't his coloring—the Skyflit family back in Pleasant Hollow had similar skin, hair, and wings—it was the way he was dressed. Instead of the simple silk and leaf tunic belted at the waist worn by everyone Shade had ever known, this sprite, who only seemed a little older than her, wore a dazzling white shirt that made his blue skin look even bluer, black pants, and a tight-fitting black leather waistcoat that matched his shiny boots. On every finger, jewel-encrusted rings glittered. "You okay?"

Shade, realizing she was staring, looked away. "Uh, yeah, I was just—"

"Overwhelmed, right?" the sprite said, flashing her a smile that included a gold tooth in the middle. "Yes, I can remember when I first came to the goblin market as a wee little shaver. Got lost and cried my eyes out until my dad finally found me. Now, I'm a fixture around here—Pyrite the Bedazzler, finest purveyor of jewelry in the kingdom! So what's your name and where are you from, little lady?"

"The name's Shade," she answered, a little leery. Physically he was, as his name stated, dazzling, but she found his manner a bit overbearing. In spite of that, his handsome features and the way he looked at her— admiringly, like someone appraising a rare and valuable gem, instead of with the disdain she was used to seeing in the eyes of the sprites of Pleasant Hollow— felt intoxicating. "And—"

"Lovely name! Just lovely! Changed or shortened it,

did you? A lass after my own heart!" Pyrite put his hand up and spoke behind it as if to conceal a secret, even though he said just as loud, "Pyrite's not my real name either, but it's a lot easier for folks to remember than those ridiculous mouthfuls we usually get saddled with, am I right?"

"*And,*" Shade continued, crossing her arms in annoyance at being interrupted while also blushing from Pyrite's compliment, "to finish answering your question, I'm from Pleasant Hollow."

"Oh, lovely village, Pleasant Hollow! Why, my uncle lives there!"

"Really?" Shade was skeptical. "What's his name?"

"Oh, you wouldn't know him," Pyrite replied with a dismissive wave of his hand. "Now, we sprites need to stick together—I wouldn't want any of the sharpies around here to think you were some bumpkin that they could take advantage of. So let me just say that, in my professional opinion, such a beautiful lady as you should be adorned with something similarly elegant and beautiful to help you shine, am I right?"

Before Shade could object, Pyrite grabbed a reddish gold necklace in the middle of which hung a leaf made of emeralds, and in an instant, she was wearing it. As the emeralds twinkled, and the gold flashed in the torchlight. Shade was convinced it was the most beautiful thing that wasn't a book that she had ever seen. "This is—"

"Just perfect for you, my lovely little acorn. Spratling!" he called over his shoulder as he continued to smile his ivory and gold smile at her, "Bring the looking glass so this lady can admire herself."

The door on the wagon opened and a squat, tired-looking kobold in dirt-stained clothes, his long, pointy ears and nose all drooping, limped down the stairs, a bronze chain clanking from his manacled ankle. "Here," he sighed, holding up a small mirror.

"See how a little dazzle can unlock a person's beauty? The gold brings out the little flecks of gold in those lovely eyes, and the green is a perfect compliment for your flawless dark skin! Am I right, or am I right?" Pyrite gushed.

Shade had to admit that he was right. Seeing herself with the necklace made her feel more sophisticated somehow. Almost regal. For the first time in her life, she felt beautiful! Part of her wished that some of the sprites she had grown up with who had made fun of her "boring mudskin" and "chubby blueberry body" could see her just then. "It certainly is beautiful—" she began.

"Catch that, Spratling?" Pyrite said, nudging the kobold, before calling out loudly, "Hey Schlumberger! The little lady loves your leaf necklace!"

A gruff voice from behind the wagon shouted, "Get donkled, ya crooked coal-chewer!"

The insult and a clanking of the kobold's chains snapped Shade out of her reverie, and she caught a brief look of disgust and rage pass over Pyrite's face. What before had seemed so handsome and winning about Pyrite now seemed sinister. She took the necklace off and held it out to Pyrite. "I'm sorry. I can't buy this. I—"

Pyrite held up his hands. "No, do not give it back! It looks too perfect on you! I insist you take it."

Shade thought about the tips from Radishbottom's book. "What's the price?"

"Oh, let's not worry about that, shall we?" Pyrite said. "What's important is making sure that something of beauty finds its place in the world, and that necklace there belongs—"

"Right here with you." Shade forced it into Pyrite's hand.

He sighed and shook his head. "So sad. So sad. Well, is there anything else I can help you with?"

"I'm looking for books. Do you know where I can find any?"

Pyrite put his arm around her shoulders, which made her squirm. "Don't see many books around this market, little lady. Best try the junk peddlers—they have a little bit of everything. Start with Sanford, over near the northern wall. If he's got nothing, come back, and I'll think of someone else for you to try and something else for you to try on that might win that heart of yours, my singularly sweet little sprite."

"Thanks." With no intention of coming back, Shade

turned to go and bumped straight into Rigoletto Ginch. The Professor, who stood next to him, smiled then hugged her, patting her vigorously on the back-pack while he did so, until she managed to push him off. "What are you two doing here? Are you following me?"

"No, of course we no follow you!" Ginch declared. The Professor nodded. "Okay, we follow you a little bit, but—"

"Thief! Thief!" Pyrite started shouting. "Security! We have a thief here!"

Shade punched Ginch in the arm. "What did you two take?"

"We no steal-a nothing!" Ginch objected, waving his arms. "He's-a try to—"

"All right, all right. What's all this then?" asked a red-capped goblin with the black fur and head of a German shepherd as he smacked a wooden club into his hand. Behind him stood a red-capped spriggan, fishing around his yellowed, jagged teeth with a tooth-pick. A crowd gathered to see the commotion.

"I demand justice!" Pyrite declared. He pointed his finger in Shade's face. "That fairy has stolen from me!"

I know, gentle Reader, I know. Here was a perfect chance for the writer to unite Shade with a fellow sprite and teach us all something about the importance of kindness and helpfulness and maybe even some interesting facts about gemology and jewelry making. And what do we get instead? Lies and treachery. Why, if I weren't contractually obligated to narrate this story from start to finish, I'd storm off in a huff! Since, unfortunately, I cannot, I encourage you to storm off in the huffiest huff you are capable of. I'll wait here until you're done.

9

In which Shade acquires a
fabulous new outfit and companions
of questionable character . . .

"What? No! I didn't—How could I—" Shade
sputtered.

"Officers, it's like this," Pyrite began,
his face taking on a look of sadness and wounded
honor. "This little sprite, who seemed so sweet and
innocent, tried to take advantage of my good nature."

"Why you—I never!" Shade shoved him. The spriggan instantly grabbed her with his long, leathery talons and held her in place.

"I regret to say it's true. Search her bag and you'll find a lovely gold and emerald necklace," Pyrite said, shaking his head sadly. The spriggan released one of Shade's arms and started rummaging through the backpack.

"Hey!" Shade objected. "I'm innocent, and he's a lying sack of squirrel scat!"

Pyrite pointed to a little hobgoblin standing nearby. "You saw her admiring that necklace, didn't you?"

The hobgoblin nodded. "Seemed quite taken with it, she did."

"Of course she was! I have the finest jewelry in the market!" Pyrite declared proudly. "She made a big fuss over it then said she had to 'think about it.' As soon as she walked away, I noticed it wasn't on my table—"

"'T'ain't 'ere," the spriggan said, shaking his head.

Pyrite frowned. "What do you mean it's not there? I put . . . I mean, Spratling here must have seen the whole thing, right?"

The gaunt little kobold looked pained. "I suppose."

"You saw her put it in her bag, didn't you?" Pyrite glared at the kobold.

"'That's-a no what happen," Ginch said quickly. "I see-a the whole thing! When the little sproot go to leave, the Pryright—"

"Pyrite," Pyrite interrupted.

"That's-a what I say. So the Pryright, he stuff-a the necklace in his pocket and start-a the yellin'! You check-a his pockets, and you see!"

"What? That's ridiculous! I would never—Hey! Get away from me, you stupid pixie!" Pyrite yelled, slapping at the Professor as he stuffed his hands in Pyrite's pockets. Pyrite gave the Professor a hard shove that sent him sprawling on the ground. In one hand, held high, was the necklace.

"See! I tell-a you!"

Pyrite grabbed the necklace out of the pixie's hand. "No! That's not—"

"It's true!" Spratling squealed. "That's exactly what happened! Arrest him!"

"Yes!" shouted a wrinkled, bearded old dwarf in a grimy blacksmith's apron as he jogged around the wagon, a bronze chain clattering on one foot and a smith's hammer clutched in one hand. "He cheats customers all the time! Brags about it and about outsmarting you officers whenever he has the chance!"

"Schlumberger! Spratling! I'm going to—Hey! Put me down, you oaf!" Pyrite shrieked as the spriggan threw Pyrite over his shoulder as he grew and grew until he towered over all the market-goers, most of whom were shouting for Pyrite's arrest, imprisonment, or dismemberment. "I pay you goblins for protection!"

"Market law's market law," the black-furred goblin declared loud enough for all to hear. Shade then heard him whisper, "You got sloppy, sprite, so we gotta make an example of you."

"'Roight. Or mebbe a meal o' ya," the spriggan whispered to the kicking and screaming Pyrite as he carried him off.

The crowd that had gathered either followed the goblin and spriggan to see what was to become of Pyrite or dispersed in search of deals and other entertainment. The dwarf and kobold laughed loudly as the dwarf knocked the chains off their legs.

Shade was so relieved she felt like she might melt. She turned to Ginch and the Professor and said, "Thank you. I don't know what would have happened if you hadn't been here. I guess it was pretty lucky that you saw him pocket that necklace," Shade told Ginch.

"He no put it in-a his pocket," Ginch said.

"What?"

"The brownie's right," Spratling said. "He planted it in your backpack."

"Then how—?"

"Oh, that's-a easy. We see-a the crooked sproot put-a the necklace in you pack, so the Professor get-a it out of the pack and in the Pryright's pocket," Ginch explained. "See—you need-a more than a book to stay out of the trouble. From now on, you stick-a with us."

"Well, I don't know. I was—" Shade started to say before Ginch and the Professor each threw an arm under each of hers and carried her off, her feet hanging an inch above the ground. "Hey!"

"Wait!" Schlumberger called.

Ginch and the Professor halted abruptly and exchanged a worried look. They turned themselves and Shade slowly around to face the dwarf and the kobold. "I'm-a sorry, but we gotta go right away to see a guy about a thing and—"

"Not before we thank you properly," Spratling said, placing the gold and emerald leaf necklace around Shade's neck. Schlumberger held out diamond and ruby encrusted rings to the other two fairies, which swiftly disappeared in their pockets. "Payment for our freedom. If there's ever anything we can do for you—"

"Then you come straight to Schlumberger and Spratling, Jewelers Extraordinaire!" the dwarf finished.

"Yeah, good luck with all of that," Ginch said as he and the Professor swiftly walked Shade away. "Now we gonna help-a you out, little sproot."

"My name's Shade."

"That's-a the fine name, little sproot. First we get-a you the new clothes."

"What's wrong with my clothes?" Shade said, looking down at her tan tunic.

"I'm sure it's-a fine for you little sproot village, but

here it lacks-a the . . . the . . . 'Ey, Professor, what's-a the word?" The Professor tilted his head back, looked down his nose at the brownie with a snooty air, and snapped his fingers. "That's-a it! You lack-a the pa-nache!"

"Panache?"

The Professor and Ginch nodded. "Yeah. You know, the style! You look-a like a rube, which is-a why we take-a you to see our favorite leprechaun."

Now I know what you're thinking: *At last, a proper fairy that isn't villainous! A red-cheeked, red-haired mis-chievous imp clad in green capering about protecting his pot of gold and reluctantly granting wishes that backfire in hilarious ways!* Oh, sweet Reader, your optimism is charming but heartbreaking, for in the store, crammed full of all manner of clothing and fabric that Ginch and the Professor dragged Shade to, sat an exceedingly overweight leprechaun with greasy black hair combed over his bald head wearing a sweat-stained white shirt and red velvet pants held up by black and white check-ered suspenders. I truly am sorry, but dreadful fairies are what I have to work with here, so dreadful fairies it must be.

Ginch gestured to the clothing, boots, and fabrics that filled the store from floor to ceiling. "Okay, little Sprootshade, meet Liam O'Buggery, the best leprechaun haberdasher in-a the world!"

"He's just saying dat," Liam groaned as he strained to get up from the stool he was sitting on, "because oi let him and dat udder bucket o' snots cheat me at cards."

The Professor smiled and fanned cards out in both of his hands. "If they cheat you, why do you keep playing with them?" Shade asked. "Seems pretty dumb to me."

"He's-a got-a the gambling problem," Ginch explained as Liam took the measuring tape hanging around his neck and held it up to Shade's arm.

"Yeah, and unloike all the udder gamblers in dis dunghole, dese two boggin' tramp-heads don't break yer arm when ye owe dem money. Dey just annoy ye half to death."

The Professor sprang across the store on his grasshopper legs and landed right next to him, pulling a slide whistle from his pocket mid-air. He gave it a few blows—Whee-oo! Whee-oo!—before the leprechaun slapped it out of his hands.

"See?" Liam sighed. "Now hold still, lass, and let me work me magic."

And magic it was to Shade, who had never seen a leprechaun make clothes for a fairy before. Like a sweaty velvet tornado, he whirled around her and the shop, grabbing clothes and fabric, throwing them on her, cutting and trimming and sewing as he went, until he finally came to a stop, panting hard.

Shade walked over to a full-length mirror in the corner of the shop and looked at herself. Instead of her simple tunic, she wore a loose-fitting tan shirt with delicate lace trimming on its cuffs and collar, a supple, forest green vest with delicate and subtle gold embroidery that cinched in at the waist and extended halfway down her thighs, below which were green pants and hard leather boots. She thought she looked strong and beautiful, like her mother had when she put on her armor and went off to war. Shade felt transformed:

the self-conscious little sprite with the courage to speak her mind but to do little more than that had been replaced by a brave, bold adventurer, ready and able to surmount any obstacle that might stand between her and her goal.

"This is wonderful!" she gasped.

The Professor skipped over, fastened the emerald necklace she thought she had hidden deep in her backpack around her neck, and then kissed his fingers. "There! The piece doo resist!" Ginch declared.

The leprechaun shoved a long, brown leather coat into Shade's hands. "Here, for when it gets nippy. Oi tink dat squares it, and oi'm rid of ye two eejits forever!"

"That's-a fine, Liam," Ginch said as they exited the shop. "We see-a you at the Thursday card game?"

The leprechaun sighed. "Aye, oi'll be dere."

Outside the shop, Ginch and the Professor drew in close to Shade. "All right, now that you look-a respectable like us," Ginch said as he and the Professor gestured up and down at their threadbare, ill-fitting outfits, "what-a you want here in Gypsum?"

"I'm looking for books," Shade replied.

The Professor reached into the back pocket of his pants and pulled out a book. The cover read "*Pick a Pocket: A History of Stylistic and Functional Design in the Field of Applied Pocketry* by Professor Lucius Theodosius Pinky."

"Thanks, but I'm looking for more than just one book," Shade said, handing it back to the Professor, who promptly tucked it in a pocket in his jacket. "I'm looking for a place where there are lots of books. Books to fill days, weeks, years, maybe even *centuries* of reading time!"

Ginch and the Professor looked at each other and shrugged. "We no know a place like that," Ginch said shaking his head. Suddenly, his eyes widened, and he snapped his fingers. "I know—we take-a you to see the Baba Ingas! If anybody know a place like that, it's-a the Baba Ingas!"

In which Shade meets and annoys
the Amazing Baba Ingas . . .

Before we get started on this chapter, I'd like to let you know that it features a witch. I tell you this in the hopes of managing your expectations a little. While it is perfectly natural for you to get excited about the appearance of a witch—what with their known tendencies to fly on cleaning equipment, eat suitably plump children, and live in edible houses (which has always seemed ill-advised to me, but to each their own, I suppose)—you should know better than to expect anything other than disappointment in this dreadful tale. And disappointing she will no doubt be.

"Here?" Shade asked, gazing skeptically at the run-down shack that squatted, seemingly on the verge of collapse, at the furthest edge of Gypsum-upon-Swathmud. Its foundation was surrounded by a ring of straw and sticks that looked like a giant nest. A weathered sign in front read:

THE AMAZING BABA INGAS
FORTUNES TOLD!
FUTURES FORESEEN!
OFFICIAL DOCUMENTS NOTARIZED!

The Professor pointed and nodded.

"This is-a the place—home to the mystical, majoostical Baba Ingas!" Ginch declared grandly. The pixie placed his battered top hat over his heart.

Shade crossed her arms. "This feels like a scam."

"After all we do for you, you think we would-a scam-a you?" Ginch asked indignantly. The Professor gave her a hurt look, dabbed at his eyes with a hand-kerchief he pulled out of his sleeve, and then blew his nose noisily into it.

"Absolutely."

The brownie and pixie shrugged. "Okay, we would," Ginch conceded while the Professor nodded energetically. "But we no scam-a you here. The Baba Ingas knows everything there is-a to know about ev-erything. You just go in and ask-a. We wait-a right here for you."

"You're not coming in?" Shade asked, suspicious.

"The Baba Ingas, she prefer to talk-a the one-on-one so there's-a more room for the spirits to come in the hut and tell-a her all that's-a hidden."

"Slug snot," Shade said.

"Fine, you tell-a the Baba Ingas that youself," Ginch replied as he and the Professor gave Shade a shove through the bead curtain hanging in the hut's doorway.

Shade stumbled into a windowless room filled with a pungent haze of incense smoke where a hundred candles burned, all of them bloodred. Flickering flames caused glass jars filled with snakes and lizards and spiders and all manner of animal and unidentifiable pulpy things to glow. Shadows of the dried plants and animal feet and bones hanging from the ceiling danced in the gloom. In the center of the room was a round table covered with a black table cloth embroidered with arcane symbols. On the table sat a crystal ball, glowing eerily.

A door hidden by one of the many multicolored drapes lining the walls creaked open to reveal a hunched old pechish woman (pechs being, as I'm sure you know, very similar looking to us, only shorter—four feet tall on average—and much stronger and magically inclined) wearing a loose peasant dress as crimson as the candles, a wide gold sash covered in jingling coins encircling her waist, and an ivory shawl draped over her shoulders. A strip of red cloth was tied over her eyes. "You come seeking answers," she wheezed in a thick accent as she slowly approached Shade. "I, ze amazing Baba Ingas, haff zem."

"Yeah, we'll see," Shade said, smirking.

"Yes, ve vill," Baba Ingas replied in her weak, cracking voice as she sat at the table. "Sit and hold out your hand."

Shade snorted and did as the pech asked. The fortune-teller took Shade's hand in hers. "You . . . seek somezing . . ."

"Wow," Shade said flatly.

"Somezing . . . you've lost . . . or haff never had . . ."

"Gee, there's no way you could have ever guessed something like that."

The old witch frowned. "To do zis, you are prepared to go on great journey—"

"Which you can easily tell by the fact that I'm wearing traveling clothes—"

"And how am I supposed to know zat ven I'm blind!" Baba Ingas snapped.

"Blind my Aunt Fannyfeather, you fraud!" Shade laughed. "I mean, how exactly are you supposed to read my palm or use that stupid crystal ball if you're blind?"

Suddenly the table started to rattle and shake and a loud rapping came from underneath. "Your impudence has angered ze spirits, little sprite!" Baba Ingas cried. "Ze only zing zat might appease zem—"

"You're doing that with a toe-ring, right?" Shade asked as she peeked under the table cloth. "Yep, there it is. And, yes, the table legs are different lengths to make it easy to move around, just like I read in that chapter of Erik the White's *A Magician Among the Spirits*. Oh, that lantern mounted on the bottom is clever though—I wondered how you were making that ball glow."

"Okay, listen you little creep," Baba Ingas growled, her accent vanishing. "If you think you can come in here and completely donkle with me then—"

"She's-a with us! Ha-ha! She get-a you good! I no think-a you can-a dupe her and-a you can't!" Ginch laughed as he and the Professor clattered through the beaded curtain. The Professor slapped his knees and then clutched his belly as he mimed laughter. A glare from Baba Ingas made him stop and try (mostly unsuccessfully) to keep a straight face.

"Watch it, *Reginald*," she said, taking off her blindfold and sweeping off her white wig to reveal chin-length black hair. Without what Shade could now tell were fake warts and makeup wrinkles, she would be quite an attractive fairy. "Remember I've known you since before you started using that ridiculous fake accent."

The Professor pointed at Ginch, who had stopped smiling, and soundlessly laughed at him. "'Ey, there's-a no need to get-a personal here! We got-a the business to conduct."

Baba Ingas took out a long-stemmed pipe and lit it with one of the many candles in the room. "On the table."

Ginch and the Professor put the rings that Spratling and Schlumberger had given them on the table, and then pulled out another twelve rings, six bracelets, nine necklaces, a couple pocket watches, and three gold teeth.

"Hey, most of that's from Spratling and Schlumberger's," Shade said. "I can't believe you stole from them after they gave us presents!"

"We no steal-a from the kobold and the dwarf! We steal-a these from the Pryright before he get arrested, so it's-a okay." Ginch turned to Baba Ingas. "She get-a the Pryright arrested today."

Baba Ingas looked impressed. "She did, eh? Good riddance. He gave us decent crooks a bad name." Baba Ingas took a silk bag out of a nearby dresser and counted out some gold and silver coins, which she stacked on the table. "Twenty gold, ten silver for the lot."

Ginch shook his head as the Professor swept the coins into a pocket in his baggy pants. "Twenty-five."

Baba Ingas frowned and flipped another gold coin at them. The pixie held his pants pocket wide, and the coin clinked down in it. "Twenty-one, but only because Pyrite gone opens up a few . . . business opportunities for me. So what's the story with your new partner here? Pretty smart for a sprite, aren't you?"

"Pretty lousy for a witch, aren't you?" Shade fired back.

"I was always better at performing than magic. Used to do an act with my two sisters: the Sisters Baba. Ever hear of us?" Shade shook her head. "Figures—you're too young. Now my oldest sister, she's really the magician of the family. Yaga used to do this bit with a trained hippogriff, a wheel of Wensleydale cheese, and a pair of long underwear that—"

"That's-a the great story," Ginch interrupted, "but the little Sprootshade here—"

"Just Shade."

"That's-a what I say. So the little Sprootshade here wants-a the books."

Ingas nudged the Professor. "Did you show her *Pick a Pocket*?" The Professor nodded.

"No. I'm not just looking for *a* book. I'm looking for a place where there are *lots* of books. Books to fill a lifetime! Somewhere a person can read to her heart's content for the rest of her life without people bothering her."

Baba Ingas studied Shade as she puffed on her pipe. "Grew up around books, did you? How many?"

"Seventy-four."

Ingas whistled. "Rare for someone not of a noble family to have that many books. Shame they all burned."

Shade started. "How did you—?"

Ingas blew a smoke ring. "Doesn't take a witch to know when someone's lost something, and unfortunately when books get lost, it's to fire and stupidity more often than not. As far as what you're looking for, there are a number of nobles, mostly elves, with big private libraries, which they'll only let their own families and friends see. And as far as the great independent libraries, folks've been burning them down for centuries."

Shade felt crushed. "So you're saying there's nowhere I can go?"

Baba Ingas's eyes softened She drummed her fingers on the table and pursed her lips. "There is one place. Maybe. Before the last war, there stood three vast repositories of books and scrolls maintained for the use of scholars, witches, warlocks, learned nobles, and officials of the Seelie Court. Two were destroyed, but the third library, as far as I know, survived."

Shade's heart raced—she *needed* that library. "Where is it?"

Baba Ingas arched an eyebrow and casually blew a smoke ring at Shade that made her cough. "Why should I tell you? What's in it for me?"

"I . . . I could tell people you're a fraud if you don't." Shade crossed her arms, trying to look tough.

Ingas's eyes narrowed. "You do that, and you're liable to have a most unfortunate accident around here."

"'Ey, ladies, there's-a no need to get-a nasty!" Ginch declared as the Professor took out a whistle, gave it a loud tweet, and held up his hands in front of the two. "Now, Ingas, she's-a no gonna grass you out. And she did-a just help get rid of the Pryright, which should mean-a the money in-a you pocket, eh?"

Baba Ingas looked back and forth from Ginch to Shade and drummed her fingers on the table. "All right! But only if you give me all the rest of your Pyrite loot."

Ginch and the Professor held out their arms and looked confused. "What-a you talk? We no know-a—"

"The rest. Now."

"Fatcha-coota-matchca, strega!" Ginch said. He and the Professor shoved their hands in their pockets and slapped a few more rings and bracelets on the table.

Ingas held her hand out in front of the Professor's face. *"All* of it."

The Professor smiled sweetly then gently spat a sapphire ring out on her palm.

"All right, then. The library lies due west, along the seacoast," Ingas said as she wiped off the Professor's ring. "To get there, you'll have to brave the dangers of the Grim Forest, then follow the coast until you come to the Marble Cliffs. The library, if it still stands, will overlook the sea from the cliffs' highest point. I can't guarantee it still exists, and I can't guarantee you'll be allowed entrance if it does, but that's your best bet of finding what you're looking for."

"Thank you," Shade said, taking her hand. Baba Ingas's whole body went rigid, and her eyes rolled back in her head.

In a ghostly voice, she sang:

> Offer shelter to the spent,
> When threatened do stand tall,
> Return the stolen innocent,
> And have forgiveness for all.
> A dangerous path lies before you,
> Hidden strength follows behind,
> In time, if you earn your due,
> That which you seek, you shall find . . .

The song complete, Baba Ingas's body relaxed. She pulled out a chair and collapsed into it. "See, I'm not a total fraud," she groaned, rubbing her temples. "Now beat it—the spirits say you've got to head out tonight if you want to succeed. And Ginch, the next time you and the Professor bring me someone looking to do anything other than fence stolen goods, I'll get my hut up on its chicken legs and have it stomp you to death!"

"And now that we help-a you out, we wish-a you well," Ginch said as he and the Professor both tipped their hats to her.

"You're . . . you're not coming with me?"

The Professor whistled, waved his hands, and shook his head. "Oh no," Ginch said firmly. "What-a you do sounds-a like the trouble. Plus we got-a the business to—"

Somewhere off in the darkened town, Shade heard someone yell, "Find those two crooks! Search every inch of the this place! We'll kill 'em!"

Ginch and the Professor exchanged a worried look then turned to Shade. "You know what? For you, little Sprootshade, the business can wait. Now run! Run from-a the business!"

The Professor and Ginch grabbed their hats and dashed off into the western darkness. After a moment, Shade, partly terrified and partly relieved, ran off to join her new travel companions. Whether to or from certain doom, she wasn't sure.

11

In which a forest is braved, a beast is saved, a road is semi-paved, and a Wild Hunt does something that, regrettably, does not end in "-aved" . . .

The three fairies ran and ran into the countryside until they were far, far from Gypsum and set up camp for the night.

"'Ey little Sprootshade, did Baba Ingas speak-a the truth?" Ginch asked as he warmed himself by their campfire. "Did alla you books burn up?"

"Yeah," Shade said, frowning at the flames. "The stupid thistlepricks in my village burned my house down with their stupid fireworks."

Ginch and the Professor's eyes widened. "And what's-a the village you from?"

"'Pleasant Hollow."

The two crooked fairies looked at each other. "Well, look at-a the time! Goodnight!" Ginch and the Professor threw themselves on the ground, put their hats over their faces, and immediately made loud snoring noises.

Shade took out Radishbottom's book and looked at it. *Books have never let me down, and while some of the stuff in you has helped, there's stuff that you don't cover and stuff you just plain get wrong. If I can't completely trust what you and other books tell me, what can I trust?*

The next morning, the three walked to the edge of the Grim Forest, its immense trees looming before them. A chill breeze blew, making Shade and the others shiver.

"You sure you wanna go in-a there, little Sprootshade?" Ginch asked uneasily.

Shade hesitated. No doubt you've read stories about kind, happy fruit trees that allow children to play in them, enjoy their fruit, and even perhaps be so selfless and so lacking in self-esteem as to sacrifice their very limbs and trunk for some child's selfish desires (thus preventing other children from having the chance to enjoy the kind little trees' generosity, but I digress). The trees of the Grim Forest were most decidedly not that kind of tree. These were immense, stern trees—their leaves and trunk so dark as to almost appear black—that seemed to threaten to break your limbs if you dared climb them, give you a bellyache if you dared to eat any of their fruit, or make a pup tent out of your skin and bones if you dared to even think about making a cottage or boat out of them.

"Yes," Shade said quietly but resolutely as she hid her trembling hands in the pockets of her jacket. "We have to. Baba Ingas said that the way was through here."

Ginch and the Professor sighed. "All right. You grow up in-a the forest, so you lead-a the way."

It was true, Shade had grown up in a forest. The Grim Forest, however, was about as different from that forest as one forest can be from another. Think of the forests that sometimes crop up in your nightmares on those nights when you decide not to read *Nanny Pleasantry's Tales of Virtue, Inspiration, and Personal Improvement* right before bed and instead pick up your older brother's dog-eared copy of *Bloodcurdling Tales of Torture, Terror, and Unpleasant Disembowelment*. Those dark, sinister forests where the leaves blot out the sun in the day and the moon in the night, where the roots trip your feet and branches scratch at your face for daring to trespass there, where every sound seems to be a shriek or a howl or a death rattle, where predators feast and little children have no hope of brave hunters or kindly fairy godmothers arriving at the last minute to save them from the wolves or the witches or the monsters or the trees themselves. The Grim Forest was *that* kind of forest.

The three trudged through the forest's undergrowth, which, fortunately for them, did not amount to much. With the sun's rays so thoroughly blocked by the dark canopy of the towering trees, little grew upon the hard earth of the Grim Forest. Still, Shade and the others often stumbled in the dark shadows of the place as they constantly looked around them, unnerved by the feeling that somebody or something was watching them at all times.

After hours of hard walking, Shade pointed to a place where the trees thinned out. "Hey, what's that up ahead?"

They hurried over to this break in the trees to discover a hard-packed dirt road. Bits of gravel suggested it had once been better maintained, and weeds growing in patches here and there showed it was now rarely used. Shade looked up and was actually able to see the cloudy gray sky above them.

"It's-a part of the King's Highway!" Ginch said happily. "Let's-a take it! I could-a kiss it, but it's-a the road and that would-a be gross . . ."

Shade had never seen the King's Highway before, the Merry Forest being a fairly isolated place, but she had read about it: a series of roads established by King

Ethelred the Wise long ago to help merchants drive their goods to market, troops mobilize for battle, and the king travel and oversee his kingdom as completely and knowledgeably as possible. "It is headed west," she said. "We could stick with it as long as it keeps going that way."

Ginch and the Professor skipped happily ahead. Shade followed, not as energetically but definitely relieved to walk on level ground and to see the sky overhead.

That relief was unfortunately short-lived. Not long into their walk, they heard a desperate yelping from the woods nearby followed by a woman's voice calling for help. From the trees raced a creature that looked like a small fox but pure white, its fur shimmering slightly as it raced toward them, its amethyst eyes wide with terror. It bounded toward the trio and reared up, placing its soft front paws on the Professor's shoulders. Its tongue lolled out as it panted with exhaustion.

Shade looked to the woods where it had come from. "Who was yelling?"

"Please," the fox-creature pleaded, its voice a soft, silky, feminine one, "you have to help me! I've been chased for weeks! First the knight! Now a wild hunt! They'll kill me! You have to help!"

The Professor nodded and looked to Shade, eyes wide, clearly hoping that she had some idea to help the creature.

"What are you? What's going—?" Shade started to ask but stopped. From somewhere nearby she heard the sound of hooves and harsh voices calling "The beast went that way!" and "Get it! Kill it!" She whipped off her backpack, unstrapped the thin briefcase Chauncey had given her, and opened it. "In here! Quick!"

The creature looked puzzled. "In there? But I'll never fit. I—"

Before the creature could finish, the Professor grabbed her and shoved her into the valise. When she had disappeared inside, the Professor looked at the bottom of the suitcase quizzically, smiled, gave Shade a thumbs-up, then slammed it shut and tucked it under his arm.

Just then a wild-eyed pony vaulted out from the forest ahead and galloped toward them, followed by four more, snorting and whinnying. Now when I say "pony," I don't mean the kindly sort that patiently gives little children safe (but quite dull) rides and ignores sticky fingers and tugs on its mane, like the one you rode at your friend Parvathi's birthday party when you were six. No, these were fierce fairy war ponies, bred and trained for combat. Come near one of them with sticky fingers, and it might well bite them off before stomping you to death.

Even more fearsome than the ponies were their riders. They were clad in black leather and dark bronze, swords clattering at their sides and long spears with wicked, barbed points clutched in their hands. Most unnerving of all were their helmets: each one was fashioned to look like the snarling, vicious face of a predator—wolf, bobcat, wolverine, bear. The leader of the hunt, helmet shaped like a shrieking hawk and armor covered in studs and spikes, reined her pony in front of Shade, and waved her spear in a circle. The other hunters slowed their ponies and came to a rest in a ring around the three.

The hawk-helmed hunter's spear tilted downward, stopping inches from Ginch's face. "We seek a rare and precious beast," the hunter said, voice echoey and muffled by the helmet. "You saw where it went."

"We see it, eh?" Ginch asked. "About this high? White-a the fur? Look-a like the fox but talk-a like the lady?"

"Yes!"

Ginch shook his head. "We no see it."

"Thistleprick," Shade groaned, covering her face with her hand.

The leader of the hunt slowly climbed down from the saddle and stepped forward, removing the hawk helmet. Underneath was an elven face, its luminous white skin framed by long silvery hair. It would have been an extremely beautiful face except for the angry red scar that began at her left ear and ran to the corner of her mouth, splitting the skin of her cheek and creating a perpetual sneer that exposed her perfect ivory teeth. "Fenris!" she called, her pale blue eyes fixed on Shade. "Catch the scent."

The hunter in the wolf helmet took it off to reveal an actual gray wolf's head. The goblin sniffed at the air. "It passed this way, milady."

"I know that!" the elf snapped. "Tell me exactly which way it went!"

Fenris climbed down and sniffed and snuffed. While he searched, the elf stepped closer and placed a leather-clad finger under Shade's chin, tilting Shade's head up. The elf's cruel face looked down at hers, studying it intently. "You . . . remind me of someone, little sprite. Extend your wings."

"What?"

"You heard me. Extend. Your. Wings."

Memories of childhood taunts flooded Shade's mind. *Blotchy, blotchy mud-wing! Ugly, ugly owl-back! Ugly-ugly owl-back!* Her face burned, and without thinking she actually did slap away the hand. "Get your hands off me, you maggot-skinned goon!"

The elf grabbed Shade by the lapels of her coat,

yanking her off her feet. "You vile little insect! You dare lay hands on the Duchess of Sighs, leader of the Wild Hunt!"

The Wild Hunt! Shade had been too surprised by a talking white fox for those words to register before, but they did now. Shade had read of the tradition of the Wild Hunt, where members of the Sluagh performed a magic ritual then rode out to find and slaughter a rare and beautiful animal and absorb its spirit. Those who interfered with the hunt rarely lived to tell the tale. *This is bad*, Shade thought. *This is really, really bad!*

The wolf-headed goblin cleared his throat. "Lady Perchta, the scent and all other signs of the beast end here in the middle of the road."

"Where did it go?" she hissed at Shade.

Shade shook her head. "No idea."

"What's in that?" asked the bear-helmed hunter, pointing his spear at the valise, which the Professor held behind his back. The Professor turned and looked over one shoulder then the other then shook his head.

"No, there! Behind your back!"

The Professor again looked over both shoulders and shook his head.

"The case in your hands!" the goblin roared, stabbing his spear in the dirt at the pixie's feet.

The Professor cocked an eyebrow and slowly brought forward the case. He pointed at it and acted surprised.

"Yes! That case! What's in it, you stupid pixie?"

The Professor held up a finger then plunged his free hand into his pants. He pulled and strained several times, grimacing as he did so, until finally there was a ripping sound, and he pulled out a pair of green underpants covered in red polka dots. He thumped them against the valise then tossed them up onto the goblin's helmet.

The goblin coughed and gagged as he swatted them off. "Great guts! When did you last wash those?"

The Professor shrugged.

"Enough!" Lady Perchta shouted. She glared at Shade. "We are the Wild Hunt. What we do . . . is *hunt*."

"And state the obvious, apparently," Shade said.

The elf flung Shade from her with all her might. Shade involuntarily flexed her wings just before crashing into Ginch.

"The Great Owl!" the elf murmured as she looked, wide-eyed, at Shade's wings. Her mouth twisted into a savage, sneering smile. "I had heard rumors of a family, but . . . Well, this will be even more gratifying than I expected."

Shade and Ginch clambered to their feet. "Why did you call me 'the Great Owl'?" Shade asked.

Lady Perchta shook her head. "I didn't."

"You did. I heard you say—"

"What I said," Lady Perchta interrupted, "is of little consequence. All that matters once a Wild Hunt is begun is the hunt. And since you prevent us from pursuing our chosen quarry, we will just have to amuse ourselves for a little while—a *very* little while—by hunting . . . *you*."

In which the wisdom of Stinkletoe Radishbottom is once again put to the test . . .

The other members of the hunt laughed at the elf's suggestion. "Should make for a fun few minutes," the wolf-headed Fenris chuckled as he climbed back into the saddle. "Trophies? I call fingers."

"Toesies," hissed the wolverine.

"Nosies," called the bear.

"Tongues," said the bobcat.

"Ears," Lady Perchta declared, smirking at the three fairies as they gaped in terror at her. "Don't worry—we'll play fair. How does sixty seconds head start before we hunt you to your deaths sound?"

"How's about sixty years?" Ginch asked.

"No."

"It would really build-a up the suspense."

"No."

"Then how's about sixty hours?"

"No."

"I tell-a you what—how's about we play-a the cards instead?" he suggested as the Professor began shuffling a deck. The elf sent them flying with a hard slap of the back of her hand. "Well, you no say-a the 'no,' so how's about we start-a with a round of Poke-a the Púca with twos, threes, and one-eyed Jacks wild?"

Lady Perchta grinned, which made the scarred cheek gap more and show more of her sharp, savage teeth. "One . . . two . . . three . . ."

"I no think we're-a gonna play-a the cards," Ginch

said, grabbing Shade by the elbow. "C'mon, little Sprootshade—we gots to skeedeedle!"

Shade's first instinct was to do as the brownie said and run, but something nagged at the back of her mind. "No."

"Whatta you mean, 'no'?! We gots to skeedeedle! The Professor and I are very, very attached to our ears, fingers, noses, and toeses!" The Professor stuck out his tongue. "Yeah! Those too!"

"Nine . . . ten . . . eleven . . ." Lady Perchta continued.

"Stop and think a minute," Shade said, undoing the straps on her backpack. "How far will we get if we run?"

"Farther than if-a we no run!"

"But we'd never get away!"

"Sixteen . . . seventeen... eighteen . . ."

Shade yanked out Radishbottom's book and frantically flipped through the pages, sweat beading on her forehead.

"What-a you do? You try to find-a the cooking suggestions for them?"

"I know I read something important about the Wild Hunt but I can't—"

"You *read-a* something!" Ginch threw up his hands, and the Professor covered his face with his. "That's-a great! We stand-a here and get-a shishkibibbled because you wanna read—"

What if he's right? she worried. *The book has been wrong before. Am I dooming us all? But what other chance do we have?*

"Twenty-two . . . twenty-three . . . twenty-four . . ."

Shade's stomach tied itself in knots as she desperately scanned page after page. "Look, we have no chance of getting away if we just run, and I know there's something in here that might help!"

"Fatcha-coota-matchca, sproot!" Ginch cried. "Because the books, they have-a been the big, big help so far!"

"Twenty-nine . . . thirty . . . thirty-one . . ."

"They've helped some, which is more than you're doing right now!" Shade shouted, hoping somehow that she was right, both to save their lives and for the satisfaction of proving Ginch wrong. "You two distract her while I look for something to save our dingle-dangle derrieres."

"Thirty-five . . . thirty-six . . . thirty-seven . . ."

The Professor and Ginch looked at each other for a moment, then shrugged. The Professor pulled a penny whistle out of his jacket and began playing a bouncy but shrill tune—"Tweet-twa-tweet-twa-toot!"—as he skipped in a circle around Lady Perchta. She frowned and continued counting.

"Forty-one . . . forty-two . . . forty-three . . ."

Shade continued her desperate search of Radishbottom's book. *Please let me be right!* she silently prayed. *I don't want to die here! And I don't want Ginch and the Professor to die here because I was wrong!*

"We're-a no gonna be ready," Ginch said to Lady Perchta, "so I call-a the do-over. You start again."

"Tweet-twa-tweet-twa-toot!" whistled the Professor.

"Forty-seven . . . forty-eight . . . forty-nine . . ."

Here! Shade spied a section entitled, "The Wild Hunt and other Dangers of Forest Travel."

"Fifty-one . . . fifty-two . . . fifty-three . . ."

"You wanna hunt, eh? Well, hows about you hunt-a the biggest game: the bargain!" Ginch pulled out a necklace and swung it in front of Lady Perchta's face. "I give-a you a good price on-a this if-a you decide to skip-a the hunting and the trophying and—"

"Tweet-twa-tweet-twa-toot!"

Shade skimmed information about origins of the Wild Hunt, historical accounts, Sluagh cultural significance—

"Fifty-five . . . Fifty-six . . ."

"Nine!" Ginch shouted. "Twenty-three! Eighty-sixteen!"

"Tweet-twa-tweet-twa-toot!"

Shade gave a little squeak, jabbed her finger on the page, and read: *Travelers who run afoul of Sluagh on a Wild Hunt should remember that those in the hunting party are magically bound to continue the hunt until an untamed beast has been slaughtered in the wild. Because of this, their ability to seriously injure or kill anyone or anything is limited solely to uncivilized areas.*

"Fifty-eight . . ."

"Umpteen! Sleven!"

"Tweet-twa-tweet-twa-toot!"

To protect yourself, take refuge in civilized areas like villages . . .

"Fifty-nine . . ."

"Eleventy-three!"

"Tweet-twa-tweet-twa-toot!"

. . . goblin markets, or on . . .

"Sixty!"

"The King's Highway!" Shade shouted. "Don't move! Stay here on the King's Highway!"

"Kill them!" Lady Perchta shouted.

Ginch swore, jumped into the Professor's arms, and closed his eyes. Shade screamed and covered her face with her hands as the goblin henchmen hurled their spears. There were four dull thuds that made the three fairies wince. After a second, all three opened their eyes to see four spears with their points buried in the dirt next to them.

"That . . . was a warning," Lady Perchta said slowly. "Now run or we'll—"

"Do absolutely nothing to us," Shade said confidently, crossing her arms. "Until you complete your hunt, you can't hurt us as long as we stay on this road."

"That's-a what the book say?" Ginch asked.

"Yep."

He took the book from her hand and kissed the cover. The Professor put his elbow up on Shade's shoulder and snapped his finger toward Lady Perchta and her hunters. "I think that means 'scram,' you grub-sucking dungballs," Shade said.

Lady Perchta drew her sword and swung it at Shade, who flinched as the point halted a hair's breadth from her nose. "I think not," the elf hissed. "Perhaps we'll just follow the three of you for a while. Perhaps we'll reach the end of the road together. Perhaps your food will run out along the way. Eventually, regardless of the reason, each of you will leave the King's Highway. And as soon as you take one single step off this road, I—"

"Will be far, far from here," declared a deep voice from the trees. Out stepped a human wearing chainmail armor topped by a royal blue surcoat with a golden lion's head embroidered on the chest. His long, curly black hair and beard were streaked with gray. He squinted his dark eyes and drew a long steel sword from the scabbard at his hip. "That is, unless thou would like the right side of thy face to match the left."

The hunters drew their swords and circled their ponies around the man. "Feel free to try, Sir Justinian," Lady Perchta said. "And speaking of symmetry, I've always preferred matching pairs in my collection. I appreciate you helping me to complete the set."

Sir Justinian gave her a grim smile. "Not today thou won't. For, while thy actions may be bound by the magic of the Wild Hunt, mine are not. And while thy bronze blade may cut me, my iron one will do far worse to thee."

Saying this, the knight swung his blade in a great circle. The riders all did their best to duck, dodge, or parry the blade, but the bobcat helmed goblin was too slow. The blade slashed through the leather covering its arm, drawing blood. The goblin immediately started clawing at the wound and shrieking in agony, which frightened its pony so that it reared up, throwing off the goblin, whose foot became entangled in one of its stirrups. The pony bolted into the woods dragging the screaming goblin behind it.

The elf leapt up onto the back of her war pony. "It is by luck alone that you and these curs survive this day, Sir Justinian. When next we meet, you will not be so lucky," Lady Perchta growled. Then she looked directly at Shade. "And make no mistake, we will meet again. Yah!"

She dug her spurs into her pony and raced off into the trees, the rest of the Wild Hunt following close behind. The knight watched them go then turned to face Shade, Ginch, and the Professor.

"And now what, pray tell, are we to do with you lot?" the knight asked, his sword still in hand and now pointed directly at the three.

In which we spend some time with a proper hero and then, of course, bid him farewell (sigh . . .)

"Um, you could maybe start by not pointing that sword at us," Shade suggested.

"Excuse me?" the knight said.

"The sword you're pointing at us—could you maybe . . . not be doing that?"

"Oh!" The knight seemed genuinely surprised by the sword in his hand. He sheathed it in the scabbard strapped to his hip and grinned sheepishly. "Terribly sorry. You know how it is—you get a sword in your hand and after a few passes, you completely forget that you're holding the lovely thing."

Shade, Ginch, and the Professor all shook their heads. "No."

"Really? Huh." The knight shrugged. "Well, anyway, you're lucky that I, Sir Justinian du Bilgewater, formerly a knight in the service of the honorable King Oberon and Queen Titania, came along when I did. And now that I've saved your lives—"

Shade held up a finger. "Actually, she was on a Wild Hunt, so she couldn't—"

"—in the proud tradition of chivalry, may I also offer you my hospitality and invite you to dine with me?" Sir Justinian continued, oblivious to Shade's words. "My squire, a superlative cook, has thrown together a tasty stew."

Ginch patted his belly. "Sounds-a good to me. Almost a-getting killed always makes-a me hungry."

Sir Justinian laughed heartily. "Me too! I thought

I was the only one! Ha-ha! Isn't it a wonderful feeling?"

"No."

The knight cupped his hands around his mouth and called, "Grouse! O sweet, loyal, diligent Grouse!"

A peevish voice replied, "Yeah? What?"

"Fetch the stew pot, bowls, and mead here!"

A loud sigh came from the woods. "Why can't we just eat at the camp?"

"Because we have guests, and it may not be safe for them to leave the road!"

"So?"

"Oh, that Grouse! Always he jests," Sir Justinian chuckled. "Hurry it along, my faithful squire!"

There was silence for a moment, followed by an annoyed, "Oh, fine!" and an unintelligible grumbling that Shade was pretty sure included some of her own favorite rude words. In time, a skinny, sulky-looking teenage boy, shaggy hair completely covering his eyes, stumbled onto the road straining to carry a large cauldron. Like Sir Justinian, he wore chainmail, although he didn't look nearly as comfortable in it. His surcoat was green with an irritable-looking white and gray speckled bird on it. He plunked down the pot, sloshing some of its savory-smelling contents on the ground, and then dropped wooden bowls that had been tucked under his arm on the ground. "There."

"Excellent, dear chum! Now would you mind fetching the mead and cups for our new friends here?" Sir Justinian asked cheerily.

Grouse sighed and trudged back into the woods, muttering under his breath. "Nothing I'd love more, you miserable old . . ."

Sir Justinian wiped off the bowls and filled them for the three fairies. Ginch and the Professor gave an appreciative sniff, raised their pinkies, and began to slurp stew from their bowls.

"Grouse's manners may still need some slight polishing," Sir Justinian said, "but his cooking is phenomenal! Puts to shame some of the finest royal banquets. Now you're probably wondering how I, a human, came to be in the service of the most wondrous Seelie Court of the fairy world."

Grouse stepped through the trees just as Sir Justinian said this, waving his hands and shaking his head and mouthing "no" just as Shade said, "I was wondering. Were you abducted as a child?"

Ignoring Grouse's groans, Sir Justinian beamed happily. "No, my fair sprite. The Seelie Court has not abducted a child in centuries. Only the Sluagh engage in the vile practice, but even they are now banned from doing it under the terms of the current truce, which is probably the only thing 'King' Julius got right. How he and Oberon could possibly share any of the same blood is . . . But enough of that! No, I have been able to see the fairy folk since I was a child, for I . . . am the *nephew* of the second most prosperous *cheesemaker* in Bilgewater! And in my young years, when witnessing a Fairy Rade, I stepped forward in awe of the Seelie Court's splendor, knelt before my lord Oberon and my lady Titania, and pledged my life and my honor in their service! And now, my good squire Grouse, why not regale these fair ones with the story of how you came into service of the Seelie Court?"

Grouse slurped loudly at his soup. "Had the stupid luck to eat a bowl of mushroom soup and then immediately find three copper coins, two heads up and one heads down, in the early afternoon of the Feast of Saint Figgymigg, then couldn't stop seeing you little jerks. I couldn't get a job as a cook like I wanted, so I started training with Sir Blabsalot here."

"And what great luck for the both of us, eh, good Grouse?" Sir Justinian said cheerily as Grouse snorted loudly. "Now, what say I regale you with some tales of my adventures to pass the time and aid the digestion during this fine repast?"

Grouse quickly swallowed the stew he had in his mouth. "Please, don't—" he started to choke out.

"Yeah, sure," Ginch agreed. "Why not?"

Grouse looked like he wanted to spit on the brownie. "What the donkle is wrong with you, you stupid little—"

"Excellent! Excellent!" Sir Justinian cried and launched into tales of bravery and battle that enraptured everyone but Grouse—wonderful, proper tales of chivalry and moral virtue and daring-do guaranteed to quicken the pulse, touch the heart, and bring tears to the eyes. Oh, dear Reader, the tales he told could themselves fill volumes, and indeed they do, but unfortunately I can tell you none of them here.

After over an hour's worth of tales (and an hour's worth of annoyed mutterings from Grouse), Shade was quite smitten with Sir Justinian, who seemed like he had stepped right out of the pages of *Le Warte d'Arty* or *Sir McGoohan and the Chartreuse Chevalier*, but something from before troubled her. "Sir Justinian," she asked, "why are you here in the Grim Forest? Are you on some mission for the Seelie Court or—"

"I no longer serve the Seelie Court." Sir Justinian's face grew gloomy. "I served wise, noble rulers once, but I refuse to serve vain, foolish ones that compromise with enemies and turn their backs on those who have served their kingdom truly and faithfully."

Sir Justinian looked off in the distance. For the first time, Shade noticed tarnished patches in Sir Justinian's bronze chainmail, the cracks in his leather boots, and the tired wrinkles in the corners of his eyes. He ran his fingers through his hair, exposing a hole and small lumps of flesh where his left ear should have been. "Oh gosh! Did Lady Perchta—?"

"She did," Sir Justinian answered gravely. "Sorry if the injury is unsightly. None who go to war come back unscarred."

Shade and Ginch fidgeted uneasily, while Grouse grudgingly cleaned up from their meal aided by the Professor, who took the opportunity to pocket several pieces of cutlery from Grouse's stock. "So her face—"

"Was done by a great warrior, lost to us in the last war. May the Great Owl have found peace in the darkness from which she struck."

Shade opened her mouth to ask about the Great Owl, but Sir Justinian continued, "But you asked why I was here in the forest. With no worthy king or queen to serve, I wander the country seeking adventure wherever it may be found. Grouse and I have come to this forest most grim to slay a fearsome beast."

Shade didn't think the little white fox creature hiding in Chauncey's valise seemed terribly fearsome, but it had said something about being chased by a knight. "What did this beast look like?" Shade asked warily.

"*Fearsome*," Sir Justinian stressed. "Wouldn't you agree, Grouse?"

"Yeah. And chasing it has been one of the dumbest—"

"Thirty feet from nose to tail, with the scaly head and neck of a serpent, the powerful, spotted body of a leopard, and the cruel, cloven hooves of an ox. Farmers in the lands surrounding the forest have lost many sheep to it over time, and I shudder to think how many human victims it has devoured! For weeks we have pursued the beast, but sadly it has vanished without a trace. You haven't, pray tell, seen the beast in your travels, have you?"

"No," Shade said, relieved that the knight wasn't hunting the seemingly harmless creature they were sheltering. Sir Justinian grimaced in disappointment; Grouse smiled for the first time.

"As I feared—we've lost the beast. But perhaps we've come upon something even better." Sir Justinian smiled and his eyes glittered. "We have found you, a motley fellowship, daring the dangers of the dark Forest Grim. Surely—"

"I don't like where this is going," Grouse muttered.

"You three heroes—"

"Please not this . . ."

"Must be on a—"

"Don't say it."

"A quest!"

"He had to say the 'Q' word . . ." Grouse sighed, looking like he had just swallowed a bug.

"Surely," Sir Justinian said excitedly, "You are on some great quest to free the kingdom of the rule of Modthryth and replace Julius with some noble redeemer, perhaps a long-lost brother of Oberon raised by a secret society of warrior monks, and—"

"No," Shade said. "We're not—"

"Oh. Well . . . then perhaps you have some magical object of great power—a necklace or ring or something—that you seek to destroy so that Queen Modthryth and the vile Sluagh Horde cannot use it to—"

"Yeah, we got-a the ring," Ginch piped up.

"You do?" Sir Justinian gasped as Grouse swore under his breath.

"No, we—" Shade began.

The Professor pulled a pewter ring out of a coat pocket and handed it to Sir Justinian. "That's-a the ring. The ring of . . . evil?" Ginch looked to the Professor, who bore his teeth and made his hands look like claws. "Savage evil! The ring of-a the savage evil!"

"Wondrous," Sir Justinian said, turning the ring this way and that. "It doesn't look like much . . . but I can feel the power emanating from it, trying to corrupt my very soul! What must be done with it?"

"Well, you gotta throw it in-a the ocean—" The Professor shook his head and made an exploding motion with his hands. "No, you gotta throw it in-a the lava—the hot, hot lava—and melt it away! Yeah, that's-a it. Now we were a-gonna go to the lava ourselves, but I like-a you face, so I give-a it to you at the very reasonable price of fifty gold—"

"My squire and I have no money, but surely—"

"You no got-a the monies? Nevermind."

The Professor grabbed the ring and tossed it over his shoulder. Sir Justinian gave a little shout.

"It's not really a magic ring," Shade said, getting up and turning to pick up her backpack.

"The Great Owl!" she heard Justinian say behind her.

"What is this 'Great Owl' business?" Shade asked. "First Lady Perchta and now you?"

"Your wings look just like hers! Are you not the daughter of Nightshriek Glitterdemalion?"

"Yeah . . . How do you know who my mother was?"

"Why, she was the Great Owl, one of the most celebrated and feared knights of the Seelie Court!" Sir Justinian beamed.

"My mother . . . the Great Owl?" Shade was stunned. As a child she knew her mother had been a soldier, but when Shade had asked her about it, her mother would only say, "I did what needed to be done. It's over and behind me and that's all anyone needs to know." And after she was gone, all Shade's father would say was, "Your mother wished to keep that part of herself private, and I will always honor that. All we need to know is that everything she did, she did to keep us and all the good fairies of the land safe."

"Yes, the Great Owl," Sir Justinian replied. "Before the last war, she left us, vowing never to take up arms again, but she returned in our hour of greatest need. While I despise this truce with the vile Sluagh Horde, things no doubt would have ended much worse had your mother not joined the fray. Ha! No wonder Lady Perchta was so eager for your blood—your mother is the one who gave her that scar!"

Sir Justinian's tales of her mother kindled a small flame of hope in Shade's chest. *If she was such a great warrior,* Shade hoped, *then maybe . . .* "Do you know what happened to my mother after the war? Did she survive? My father and I never knew what became of her."

The knight shook his head. "The last anyone saw of her was during the battle of Stormfield. The Seelie forces were beset on all sides. Her body was never found, but few survived the onslaught. I'm sorry."

Shade's heart sank. She had always dreamed that somehow her mother was alive somewhere out in the world and would someday find her way home. Now that dream, it seemed, was dead.

"But there is hope for the world, for you, the Great Owl's daughter, lives!" Sir Justinian said. "And now that I know of your noble lineage, I'm certain you and your boon companions must be on some grand quest!"

The Professor grinned and pulled a red balloon out of his coat. "He said-a the 'boon,' not the 'balloon,'" Ginch explained. The pixie took out a pin and popped it.

"Pray tell what great adventure takes you through the Grim Forest. Perhaps I might partake in it?"

"Please don't be anything dangerous . . ." Grouse mumbled, shutting his eyes.

"We're just looking for books," Shade said.

"Yes!" Grouse said.

"Books, eh?" Sir Justinian looked disappointed for a moment but then brightened. "Surely these are books of magic meant to purge the land of—"

"No," Shade said.

"Then books full of secrets that must be destroyed lest—"

The Professor whistled and shook his head "no."

"Then what—?"

"I just want to read them," Shade said.

"Read them?"

"Read them and enjoy them and not be bothered while I do," Shade said decisively.

"Yes!" Grouse leapt to his feet and raised his fists over his head. "Winner!"

"Oh." Sir Justinian was crestfallen. "Then I suppose this is goodbye."

"Wait, what?" Grouse pointed at the three fairies. "What about joining them?"

"They need not our help, good squire. Let us see if

we can find the trail of the great beast or some other threat more worthy of our attentions."

"Oh, come on!" Grouse said. "What if Lady Perchta comes after them. Or . . . or . . . what if they're lying, and they really are after books of magic!"

"We're not—" Shade began.

"Shut up! Sir Justinian, I vote that we—"

"I am the knight, and you are my squire—there is no voting." Sir Justinian turned Grouse toward the trees and gave him a shove. "Lady Glitterdemalion, Signore Ginch, Professor—I wish you all well. If ever you need aid, call out, and if I am within earshot, I shall come. But for now, fare thee well. Adventure awaits!"

With a wave, a wink, and a laugh, he dashed into the trees, possibly never to be seen again in this book and taking with him what was most likely our only chance of proper, rousing, morally improving action and adventure. Now I know you may be eager to turn the page and see what happens next, but if you could please give your poor narrator a moment to come to grips with this sad, sad loss first, I would greatly appreciate it.

14

In which there are questions, qualms, and a Questing Beast . . .

O nce Sir Justinian was gone (sigh), and Shade, Ginch, and the Professor were quite certain they were alone, Shade unclasped the thin valise and whispered, "You can come out now. The coast is clear."

"Must I?" a faraway voice called. "It's so lovely in here. The sun, the sand . . ."

"Come on out," Shade insisted. "I want to ask you a few questions."

"Very well," the voice sighed.

Shade opened the briefcase wide, and a gigantic serpent's head, all emerald scales and slitted purple eyes at the end of long, snakey neck, rose slowly out of it. In its mouth was a thin bamboo stalk that led down to a half coconut balanced on top of a cloven ox hoof. "I hope you've tried these," the serpent said, taking a sip, "because they are deli—"

Shade let out a sharp cry and dropped the valise. When it hit the ground, all thirty snakey, leopardy feet of the creature, perfectly matching the description given by the perfectly wonderful Sir Justinian, bounced out. "My drink!" it moaned, looking sadly at its now empty coconut shell rolling in the dirt.

The Professor jumped into Ginch's arms and started pointing and whistling sharply. "That's-a the knight's creature!" Ginch gasped. "Ey, Justinian! We got-a you—"

"Shh! Shh! Shh!" the creature shushed and clasped its front hooves together. "Please, please, please don't tell him I'm here! I'm so tired of running, I might just let him slay me and be done with it if he comes!"

Shade held up a hand to silence Ginch and the Professor. "What happened to the little white fox?" she demanded.

"I *am* the little white fox," the beast explained in the same soft, lovely voice that she had as a fox. "Of my two forms, that's the one that best suited the Wild Hunt's quest to kill something beautiful and rare. While I was enjoying a nice drink by the ocean in that case—which I love by the way!— all that fur made me hot, so I switched over to this form, which is the one I was trapped in whenever Sir Justinian was nearby. I only get to choose how I look when I'm alone, I'm around people who are already occupied with specific quests, or I'm around people who don't want to quest at all."

"What are you?" Shade asked.

"I prefer 'who,'" the beast said, sounding a little hurt. "My name is Glatisant—Glatis to my friends, of which I count you since you saved my life—and I am a Questing Beast."

"And what's-a that?" Ginch asked. The Professor tapped him and put his hand at waist level and then hugged himself. "And the Professor, he wants-a to know if you could-a be the fox again—he thinks-a you cuter that way."

"Well, thank you. I should be able to change," Glatis said, the scales on her cheeks blushing slightly. She closed her eyes, her jaws clenched, and then . . . Well, you know when you reach into a sock that's inside-out and pull it so that it's right-side out? That's something like what the Questing Beast's transformation looked like—it was as if she turned herself inside out and suddenly was a little white fox again. The Professor clapped and scratched her behind the ears.

"Oo, that's nice! To answer your first question, a Questing Beast magically inspires people who are desperately seeking something—a grand quest, a great adventure, rare prey, hidden treasure, and so forth—but don't have a very specific goal in mind to chase her."

"Sounds a-tiring," Ginch said.

"Oh it is! Most Questing Beasts really enjoy being

chased, but I've always *hated* it. Unfortunately there are only three ways to end the chase once it's begun: get so far away from the pursuer that they can't find you, lead them to something that better fits what they really want, or . . ." Glatis gulped and looked ill, ". . . kill or be killed by them."

"That's terrible," Shade said. She felt sorry for Glatis, but something stirred deep in her heart. It was a desire to . . . to . . . chase the Questing Beast! *Perhaps this creature should be captured after all,* she thought. "But Sir Justinian said that you've been slaughtering sheep. Maybe worse."

"I've never harmed fairy or human or any thinking creature," Glatis said, placing a paw on her chest as if deeply wounded by the suggestion. "As for sheep . . . well, I do like a nice spot of rare—and by rare I mean still bleeting—mutton, but then who doesn't?"

As Glatis explained this, Shade broke out in a sweat. Her hands started to open and close involuntarily, as if preparing to grab something.

The fox creature yelped and jumped into the

Professor's arms. "You're going to chase me! I can see it in your eyes. Oh please don't! I'm so, so tired!" The Professor covered her with part of his coat and nodded for Shade to go away.

"I'm . . . I'm so sorry!" Shade was shocked and appalled by her overwhelming instincts. "I don't know what's happening."

"You want something desperately, but you aren't certain enough about what it is or how to get it," Glatis moaned, peeking out from the Professor's coat, "so you're going to start chasing me!"

"No, I . . . I . . . I don't want to," Shade stammered, the need to chase Glatis building and building. "How do I stop this?"

"I already told you," Glatis sobbed, "there are only three things, and I'm too tired to—"

The Professor started whistling sharply and pointing at the briefcase. *Tweet! Tweet!* Point. Point. *Tweet! Tweet!* Point!

"He wants-a you back in-a the bag!"

"Yes!" Shade said. "Nobody—Sir Justinian, Lady

Perchta, me—wanted to chase you when you were in Chauncey's vacation!"

"Could I?" Glatis wiped a tear away with a soft, snowy paw. "That would be wonderful! If I could just have a day or two—maybe a week—in there without anyone—"

"Go! Just go!" Shade cried. The Professor gave Glatis a little kiss on the head, dropped her into the bag, and waved energetically.

"Oh, thank you! Thank you! I'll never forget this!" Glatis called out. As soon as she snapped shut the case, Shade slumped, relieved of her need to chase the Questing Beast.

For the rest of the day and for most of the next, the three walked the King's Highway as it ran west, camping along its edge under dark, sinister trees during the long night and keeping a diligent watch in case Lady Perchta returned, which seemed even more likely now that Shade knew her mother was responsible for the elf's hideously scarred face. As they traveled, Ginch told jokes and stories of his and the Professor's gambling and trickery, and the Professor played his tin whistle as well as a mandolin, small harp, and set of bagpipes that he improbably pulled from various pockets in his baggy clothes. The two could be enjoyable company, Shade decided, but still she spent most of her time brooding.

Why didn't Mom ever tell me she was a war hero? And why didn't Dad ever tell me anything? Are there other secrets they hid from me? And now I have an enemy— probably an archenemy—because of Mom! Oh sweet St. Figgymigg, is Lady Perchta going to hunt me to the ends of the earth like Captain Ishmael in Sir Melville de Acuchnet's Captain Ishmael's Ill-Advised and Ill-Fated Pursuit of the Albino Whale that Bit Off His Pinky-Toe, Featuring Extensive Passages on Whaling Lore? *(Great book, but it really needs a shorter title, like maybe just the name of the whale.) And what about that thing with poor little (and sometimes immense) Glatis? It was starting to feel like I would have chased her like I was Captain Ishmael. All because I want to be surrounded by books again.*

Shade said nothing of this. Instead she listened to Ginch's songs and stories and laughed at his and the Professor's jokes and played card games (which she always lost because the two cheated outrageously). This cheered her spirits somewhat and at times took her mind mostly off her troubles, which is sometimes the most that any of us can ask for.

In which there are rants, rats, and
rescues . . .

L ate the next day as the sun began to set, the road
turned south and the three were faced with a
dilemma: Play it safe and stay on the road or
follow Baba Ingas's instructions and continue west
into the trees and risk attack by the Wild Hunt. A
slight disagreement ensued.

"Fatcha-coota-matchca, sproot! You wanna get us all
killed!"

"Listen you crooked, cardsharping con artist—Baba Ingas said the library is to the west, so we head west!"

The Professor took out a slide whistle. *Twee—ooo Ooo-weet!*

"No! We go the safe route! I no wanna have to save-a you no more!"

"Save me? When have you—"

Twee-ooo!

"'Ey, we figure how to keep-a you from a-running around after the little big fox-snake-leopardy thing until you drop!"

"I would have worked that out on my own," Shade huffed, crossing her arms. "If anything, I'm the one who keeps saving you! If it weren't for me, Lady Perchta and her goons would be wearing the two of you as necklaces!"

Twee-ooo! Ooo—

"Shut up!" Shade roared at the Professor as Ginch grabbed the whistle and snapped it over his knee. The Professor's jaw dropped in outrage, and he shoved

Ginch. Ginch shoved him back. The Professor lifted his hands up to fight. Ginch did the same. Then the Professor pulled back one hand as if to strike but instead kicked out with his foot, hitting the brownie in the seat of the pants.

"You go downstairs, eh? Well, I'm-a go upstairs!" Ginch tackled the Professor, and the two wrestled around on the ground.

"Okay, nitwits—try not to kill each other. Or do. I don't really give a saucer of snake spit one way or the other!" Shade grabbed the backpack straps resting on her shoulders and stomped off into the trees. "You'd probably just have slowed me down!"

"No, wait! That's-a no good!" She heard Ginch yell behind her. "Sprootshade, come-a back—Oof! Get offa me, you—Ow! 'Ey Sprootshade, we wait-a right here and when you come-a to you senses—Ouch! Fatcha-coota-matchca, pixie!"

Shade trudged for a long time as the already dark forest grew darker and darker as the sun went down. As the light faded, so did her anger and her resolve.

The indignant thought *Why couldn't those stubborn thistlepricks have come with me!* finally gave way to the uneasy, somewhat guilty question *How could I have left those thistlepricks behind?* Shade had spent most of her life without friends and had always thought that was completely fine—even preferable to the hassles of dealing with other folks. But just then, alone there in the Grim Forest, she realized that she had grown fond of the silly, crooked, but good-natured duo. *Maybe I was too hard on them. And maybe they were right— leaving the road was a terrible idea.*

With the last glowing embers of dusk providing the most meager of light, Shade headed back, hoping she would be able to find her way back to Ginch and the Professor but dreading having to apologize for losing her temper.

After only a few steps, however, she froze in her tracks. She heard a loud rustling, as if hundreds of dried leaves were being trampled, and odd, unnerving sounds of panting and low growls. As she wondered what could be making such noises, she heard a sharp cry, followed by shrill whistles, and finally "Hey, get-a you paws off-a me, filthy ratti!"

Shade tiptoed as fast as she could and spied Ginch and the Professor in a small clearing, surrounded and pinned to the ground by huge rats almost as big as they were. The pixie and brownie struggled to free themselves, but strong clawed paws gripped cloth and flesh, making escape impossible. The rats gnashed their teeth and hissed, "Eat! Eat! Bite! Rip! Tear! Eat!"

"No, brothers and sisters! No!" a chorus of five voices called in unison. On the far edge of the clearing, Shade saw five rats atop a stump, standing on their hind legs with their forepaws all in the air. Hanging over the edge of the stump was a complex tangle of hairless, scaly tails. "Remember the rewards promised us!"

"Meat! Meat!" the rats hissed.

"Yes! More meat than this if we give them to the Lady of the Hunt!"

Perchta! Shade thought. *She can't do anything to us yet, so she's siccing rats and who knows what else on us!*

"But we are missing one," the rat chorus said. "Where is the moth girl? Tell us, and we may be merciful."

"The moth girl?" Ginch asked.

"Yes. Above all, we were told to capture the fairy with the owl-faced wings."

"About my height? Black hair? Brown skin? Same color butterfly wings?"

"Yes!"

Shade held her breath. *After how mean I was to him, I don't blame him if he—*

"I no know any moth girl. 'Ey, paisan! You know-a the moth girl?"

The Professor shook his head.

"Sorry, Braidy, but we no know any moth girl."

"Braidy?" the joined rats all hissed.

"Yeah. You got-a the tails all a-braided together, so I call-a you—"

"You will call us by our true name and royal title: Rí Francach."

"So, you're-a the king of the rats, and you no like-a the name 'Braidy'?"

"Yes!"

"Too bad, because you're-a Braidy, the Rat King! Braidy, the Rat King!"

"Silence!" they hissed.

"Braidy, the Rat King!" Ginch chanted as the Professor began to whistle along. "He's-a Braidy, the Rat King! Braidy, the Rat King!"

"Silence them, my subjects!" the Rí Francach shouted. Rats near Ginch and the Professor sank their teeth into their arms. The Professor grimaced, and Ginch shrieked in pain.

Shade racked her brains but couldn't think of anything she had ever read that would help her just then. She wasn't capable of feats of strength like Queequeg or nimble combat like Sir Percy Dovetonsils, and none of the chivalric adventures in *Le Warte d'Arty* involved hordes of giant, semi-intelligent rats. For the first time in her life, she felt as though all her reading had utterly failed her.

"Now," the rat king's five voices hissed. "Tell us where the moth girl is!"

"I . . . I tell-a you . . ." Ginch murmured. The Rí Francach fell down upon all fours (all five sets of them) and craned its heads forward. "I tell-a you . . . I tell-a you that . . . you're-a Braidy, the Rat King! Braidy, the Rat King!"

The rats bit and clawed at them. Ginch shrieked in agony. Shade panicked. *Why couldn't I be a warrior like my mother? I don't even own a sword, much less know how to use one! If only I were the Great Owl and—wait! That's it! I'm not the Great Owl, but I can become . . .*

Shade braced herself, prayed to Saint Eeyore (patron saint of lost causes) that her lifelong lack of practice wouldn't doom her, then flapped high into the trees above and began making her best owl hoots. From her perch high up in an immense ash tree, she saw the rats start and look about nervously. "Owl? Owl? Snatchy, rippy, killy owl? Where? Where? Where?" they gibbered.

She took a deep breath and let out the loudest, fiercest hoots she could and flexed her wings to their full span, the black, brown, gray pattern with its twin rings of yellow on her back looking a great deal like the face of an immense owl glaring down at the rats.

Shade heard hisses and shrieks of "Beakses and talonses! Beakses and talonses! Run, run, run!" She peaked over her shoulder to see the rats racing out into the forest.

"Stop our subjects! Stop!" The rat king cried. "We, the Rí Francach, command—Aaagh!"

The five bodies of the rat king fell from the stump to crash in five different places on the ground. In the center of the stump now stood the Professor, grinning his silly grin, a meat cleaver from Grouse's food preparation set in one hand and five severed rat tails braided together held high in the other.

"Our . . . my . . . tails . . . separate . . . not knot . . . I, we, us, me can't . . . not francach, just francaigh . . . I, we, us, me, you can't . . . can't . . ." the five rats that were formerly one all babbled as they wandered, dazed, into the dark night.

Seeing that the last of the rats was gone, Shade

glided down from her tree. She had hoped to make a graceful and dramatic landing right in front of Ginch and the Professor but, as is often the case when we are doing our absolute best to be graceful and dramatic, failed miserably and instead crashed into them. All three fell in a tangled heap on the ground.

"Little Sprootshade!" Ginch cried. "You're alive! And-a you save us! That was-a the great, great trick! Right, Professor?"

The Professor nodded. He reached into his pants pocket and pulled out a roll of parchment tied with a red ribbon and placed it in Shade's left hand while he shook her right. Shade arched an eyebrow and unrolled the paper. It read, *Certification of Extreme Cleverness. University of Streüseldorff.* "Thanks, I guess . . ." she said.

"C'mon!" Ginch said. "Let's-a run for it! We got-a the rats and-a the hunts and-a who knows what else in-a the woods! We gotta scram!"

"I couldn't have said it better myself," Shade agreed as the three grabbed each other's hands and dashed deeper into the woods.

In which a friendship is put to the test . . .

For hours they ran, hand-in-hand-in-hand, through the darkness, their way lit only by stray rays of moonlight peeking through the canopy of leaves and the occasional flashings of fireflies. Whenever their energy would flag, the chirps and screeches and howls of the forest filled them with fresh terror to speed them along. More than once, Ginch urged Shade to fly ahead, but she would have none of it. While feeling more confident about her flying abilities thanks to their run-in with the rats, Shade wasn't sure fast flight in the dark was such a good idea. Besides, now that she had reunited with her friends, she didn't believe that she would ever want to leave their side again.

Eventually, they had to stop for breath and to clutch the stitches in their sides. Between pants, Shade heard something: a faint, rhythmic roaring. "Do you hear that?"

"What? My heart? Yeah, it go 'a-boom, a-boom, a-boom, a—'"

"No. Listen."

Ginch listened. His eyes lit up. "C'mon!" he said, grabbing his fatigued companions and dragging them toward the sound.

In short order they could see light and open sky ahead. They quickened their pace and stumbled out of the forest. Bathed in the moonlight, they saw a vast, shimmering expanse of water. White-capped waves rolled in and crashed against rocks, sending frothy spume flying into the air. Shade, who had only ever read about the ocean in books, was overcome by the beauty of water stretching all the way to the horizon. The Professor dropped to his knees and kissed the ground before sticking his tongue out and making a rude gesture at the trees.

As much as the three wanted to collapse right where they stood, they forced themselves on and found a spot further down the shoreline where large rocks blocked the cold ocean breezes and provided cover from any eyes that might lurk in the night.

"I'll get wood for a fire," Shade offered. "Then we can eat a little and get some sleep. Boy, do we need it . . ."

"Sounds-a good," Ginch agreed, sitting and stretching.

As Shade left, she could just hear Ginch saying, "I know we got-a . . . Whatta you mean tonight? That's-a no good. We wait until . . ."

Shade wanted to creep closer and eavesdrop, but she was cold and wanted a fire more. *Besides*, she thought, *we're friends. They wouldn't keep anything important a secret from me, would they?*

Once the three had a nice fire warming them, while Shade devoured an almond torte that Chauncey had packed for her (now rather stale but still quite delicious).

The Professor nudged Ginch and nodded toward Shade. "Yeah, I know," Ginch muttered. "Uh, listen, little Sprootshade, we got-a the something to tell-a to you."

"Yeah?" Shade said, picking up a waterskin.

"Well, you see . . . The ocean! Boy, she's-a pretty!"

"Mmm-hmm," Shade agreed as she drank.

After a sharp elbow from the Professor, Ginch continued, "And, uh, you see, we kinda . . . sorta . . . maybe . . . a little bit . . . burn-a you house down."

Shade choked and sprayed water all over the brownie and pixie. "What?!?"

The Professor pulled out a pair of handkerchiefs and handed one to Ginch, who started to wipe himself. "Well, it's-a like this. We were in-a Bilgewater, and we find-a the bunch of fireworks that somebody lose—"

The Professor shook his head and waggled his finger at the brownie. "'Ey, the owner lose it after we take it, so that's-a no the lie. Anyways, for personal reasons, we leave-a Bilgewater quick and go through the Murray Forest—"

"That's 'Merry' Forest," Shade said through gritted teeth. She could feel a deep, deep rage growing inside, burning hotter and hotter like a blacksmith's forge stoked by the bellows.

"That's-a what I say. So we go through the Murray Forest and we meet-a these sproots, and we make-a the trade and skeedeedle, but we warn-a them that they're-a dangerous and—"

The Professor shook his head.

"Whatta you mean we no warn them? We tell-a them—"

"You told them that they were 'perfectly safe.'" Shade's teeth began to grind. "That's what Chieftainess Flutterglide said."

"I no think I—" Ginch stopped as the Professor nodded vigorously and pointed at Shade. "Okay, maybe I say that, but what kind of the doof no know that fireworks—"

"The kind of dingle-dangle doof that I grew up with, that's who!" Shade shouted. "You gave a bunch of dangerous pyrotechnics—"

"We no give-a nobody pirate-a nothing!"

"Pyrotechnics! Fireworks! You gave dangerous fireworks to a bunch of dingle-dangle-donkled dimwits, and they burned my house down with them!"

"And we're-a sorry. We feel-a like . . . like . . ." The Professor pulled out his horse picture and pointed to its bottom. "Yeah, we feel-a like those."

"I don't care how you feel! Because of you, I lost my home! My books! My . . . my . . . my everything! And all this time, you knew!"

"Well, I wanna tell all the time, but the Professor, he say 'no.'"

The Professor's jaw dropped, and he shoved Ginch off the rock they were sitting on. Ginch jumped up and shoved the Professor off the rock, and in no time at all, the two were wrestling around on the ground. Shade got up and grabbed her bag.

"'Ey, where you go, little Sprootshade?" Ginch asked

as the Professor struggled to get out of the headlock Ginch had him in. "It's-a dark and-a dangerous and-a—"

"I don't care how dark and dangerous it is—I'm leaving!"

"Wait! We come-a with you!" Ginch and the Professor broke and scrambled to their feet.

"No, you don't! We're through!"

The Professor looked at the ground and scratched in the pebbles there with his foot. Ginch held up his hands. "Now, let's-a just calm-a down and—"

"No! I will not calm down! And I will not spend one more second surrounded by a silly, stupid pixie—"

The Professor shook his head and pulled out a scroll that read "The University of Streüseldorff hereby bestows upon the Bearer of this Diploma the degree of Doctor of Philosophy." Shade snatched it, crumpled it, and threw it in the fire.

"And a no-good—"

"I'm-a little bit good," Ginch muttered.

"Two-bit—"

"I'm-a worth at least the four bits."

"Lying—"

"I'm-a truth-challenged."

"Cheating—"

"I play-a by the alternative rules."

"Thieving—"

"That's-a fair."

"Slug-licking—"

"Just-a the one time . . ."

"Sorry excuse for a Brownie! I never want to see either of you ever again!" Shade roared. Shade spat on the ground. She stomped off. She turned her back on them and ran, tears streaming down her face. When she heard the two calling after her, she gave a mighty flap of her wings and soared into the ocean air, leaving them far behind, which is exactly where she hoped they would stay for the rest of her life.

17

In which a baby proves to be more trouble than it's worth (as they usually do) . . .

Shade wanted to fly for days until any chance she had of ever seeing Ginch and the Professor would be long gone, but the cold ocean winds buffeted her so that she was forced to give up soon after she started. She landed, stumbling, near a cottage on a low cliff overlooking the sea. Taking shelter behind a barn, Shade cursed her luck, her inability to fly better, and, most of all, her former companions. *I don't need them!* she thought. *I'll be much better off on my own, just like I've always been.*

The feelings of loss and betrayal crashed over her like the white-capped waves of the sea on the nearby rocks, and she sobbed deeply, the sort of all-body, soul-emptying sob that comes when we fully give ourselves over to heartbreak.

When the tide of her sorrow finally ebbed, she was puzzled to still hear crying. She crept along and peered around the edge of the barn. A hyena-headed goblin, a tall wolf-headed wulver, and a leathery-skinned spriggan, all wearing red caps, were gathered around a squat, warty, green-skinned, pot-bellied little bald man with a pig's snout and short horns poking out from his forehead. The little green man was clad in a diaper, held a smoldering cigar in his hand, and cried and fussed, sounding just like your baby sister Letitia does any time you've become really engrossed in a good book (as opposed to reading a book like this one, in which case a squalling infant should be a pleasant distraction).

"Das ist gut!" the wulver said, nodding approvingly.

"'Course it's good, youse mooks!" the little man replied in a deep, raspy voice. "I know my bidness!"

"We just need to make sure you got your act down before we do this job," the hyena-head goblin said. "So let's see the baby body."

The little man took a couple puffs of his cigar and then began to shudder and shake violently. Amidst the convulsions, his skin began to lighten, his features soften, his horns retract into his skull. When it was all done, there he stood, looking exactly like a human baby. "'There ya go, pally," the changeling said, chomping on his cigar with now-toothless gums. "Ya wanna a baby—bam!—ya gotta baby!"

"All right, let's do this," the goblin said, clapping his hands together. The sinister troop of fairies crept—or, in the case of the changeling, toddled—to the house and crouched under a shuttered window. As Shade watched, the spriggan began to inflate, its droopy, wrinkled skin filling up and drawing taut, until it towered over the others. The wulver picked up the changeling and handed him up to the spriggan, who lifted him up to the window, opened the shutters, and dropped him inside. After a moment, a tiny pair of hands handed a baby, completely identical to the changeling, out to the spriggan.

Watching all of this, Shade forgot her own problems and worried instead about the infant. *They're stealing that poor baby!* Shade thought, covering her mouth to stifle a cry of horror. *But Sir Justinian said that was completely outlawed! Somebody has to stop them!*

Knowing that she must do something but with no idea what or how, Shade silently trailed the red-capped gang to a copse of trees further along the cliffs. She watched as they approached a campsite where a hyena-headed goblin identical to the first tended a fire. "You get it, brother?" he asked, picking his teeth with a small chicken bone.

"We got the little beastie, Laffer," the identical goblin declared, holding up the baby who peered about and burbled.

The other goblin made a face. "*Disgusting.* Put it in the cage so it doesn't crawl away, Gaffer."

"Right." The brother handed the baby to the wulver, who walked to the edge of the camp where a large metal cage, big enough to hold a couple hunting dogs, sat. He opened the hinged top panel and lowered the baby to the bottom. The baby immediately rolled over, sat up, and rattled the cage.

"Vy boss vant kinders?" the wulver asked, joining the others around the fire. "Very little meat on bones."

"She's not gonna eat the thing, Wolfgang," Laffer explained as he handed out cups and filled them from a wineskin hanging around his neck. "She or somebody else is gonna take that thing, pay us very well for it, and then raise it up to be a warrior for the Sluagh."

"'At little fing's gonna be a warrior?" the spriggan sneered. "Oi could squish it 'tween me toes wivout 'alf tryin'."

"Give it time, Struggs," Gaffer replied. "Eventually that thing'll be as big as Wolfgang over there, *and* it'll be able to swing around *iron weapons*—"

"In the service of our noble Queen Modthryth," Laffer interrupted. He held up his cup. "Long may she reign."

"As long as the money's good!" Gaffer added.

"And the drinks are strong!"

They all laughed and drained their cups, refilled them, and drained them again as Shade watched from a safe distance. *If I wait a little and they drink enough, maybe I can sneak the baby away and back to his parents,* she thought.

Drink enough they did. Cup after cup of wine gurgled down their throats until every one of them was loud and loopy and stumbly.

When she thought the gang suitably distracted (and wobbly), Shade crept over to the cage, stood on her tiptoes, and ever so quietly opened the top of the cage. She tried lifting it to see if she could tilt it onto its side, but with the baby inside (who cooed at her) it was too heavy. *No sweat. I'm getting good at flying,* Shade told herself as she fluttered up and dropped into the cage. *I'll just grab the baby and fly it on ho—ugh!*

It was then that Shade realized that while flying may not be that hard, flying while carrying a sizable load is, and flying with a baby almost as big as you is impossible. Shade couldn't even pick up the baby, let alone airlift him out of the cage. She also learned (just as you did when you were three and they brought your little brother home from the hospital all red and wrinkly and wrapped up like a burrito) that if you grab a baby that doesn't know you and start poking it and prodding it and try to yank it up by its clothes, it will scream and cry. Quite loudly.

"Shh! Quiet!" Shade whispered as the baby wailed. "I'm saving you, you stupid baby, so shut up!"

Babies, however, are notorious for not shutting up when you kindly ask them to, and this boy was no exception. In spite of Shade's best efforts to calm him (which, let's be frank here, were not very good and mostly consisted of her patting him roughly and muttering words under her breath that would make sailors blush), the baby's cries were so shrill and piercing that Shade had no idea that the spriggan had come over to see what the trouble was until he slammed the top of the cage down.

18

In which things go from bad to
better to much, much worse . . .

"Larfer! Garfer! Come see what oi caught!" the
spriggan called.

"Wuzzat?" Laffer shouted. The goblins
and wulver stumbled over to the cage.

"Vas ist das?" Wolfgang the wulver asked, peering
blearily at Shade. "Ein sprite?"

"Now what is a sprite doing in our cage?" Gaffer asked.

I've got to think of a story and quick, Shade thought. "Um, I was . . . just . . . uh . . ." *Stupid brain! If Ginch were here he'd be on his third or fourth lie by now.*

"She were troyin' to steal our baby, she were," the spriggan said before licking at something black and rotten-looking stuck between his teeth.

"What? No! I was just . . ." *Think. What stupid reason could a sprite have for . . .* "He's . . . on my acorn . . . and I was trying to get him off!"

"What acorn?" Laffer asked as he and his brother both put their hands on their hips and cocked their heads back.

"The acorn I was tossing! Yes," Shade continued, trying to sound like one of the more air-headed sprites she knew back in Pleasant Hollow. "I was practicing my acorn tossing. I mean, you can't really expect to be great at acorn tossing if you *only* toss them when you're playing acorn toss—you've got to toss all the time, giving a 111% tossing effort every time you toss even when it's just tossing for funsies instead of a serious, league-level tossing, right? So I was tossing—111% tossing—and I missed, and it fell in the cage, and then your larval human rolled over on it and I was just trying to—"

"Vy toss in die nacht?" Wolfgang asked pointing to the sky.

"Um . . . I'm in a . . . acorn toss . . . night league? I mean, sure you can just play games in the day, but if you really want to take your acorn tossing to the next level, you need—"

"Oi!" The spriggan, who had circled around the cage, exclaimed. "You've got the bloody Owl's markin's, you 'ave!"

"Owl?" Gaffer asked.

"The Great Owl! The one what done the boss's face, roight?"

Done the boss's face? Shade's blood ran cold. *Oh, no! They work for—*

"Well, Perchta will definitely want to get a look at you when she comes, owl-back," Laffer said as he snapped a padlock on the top of the cage.

"But . . . but . . . I was just . . . tossing acorns," Shade stammered.

"Yeah? Well, I don't give an acorn toss what you were doing," Gaffer laughed. "You're ours until the boss shows up, at which point you're hers if she wants you, and Struggs's to eat if she don't."

The spriggan grinned and drooled a little. "Taste loik chicken, sproits do, wiv a noice buggy finish."

Shade shook the bars of the cage and slammed herself against the top as the baby wailed. "Let me out!" she screamed.

Wolfgang tapped Gaffer's shoulder. "Maybe ve get bonus for ein sprite, ja?"

Shade racked her brains for something she could do to save herself but could think of nothing. *If only I had help. If only I had—*"Sir Justinian! Sir Justinian! If you can hear me, help! Help!"

"Scream your head off if you want," Laffer said. "Ain't nobody around for miles to—"

"'Ey!" someone shouted from over by the campfire.

The goblin gang and Shade all turned. *It's him! It must be him!* Shade exulted. *He heard my calls for help!*

A figure stepped out of the shadows and into the

light of the campfire. It was a small figure in a too-tight brown suit with a red cap pulled over the top of his short-brimmed brown hat. In his hands, he shuffled a deck of cards. "Anybody wanna play-a the game or two?"

"Ginch?" Shade whispered under her breath. *What the donkle is he doing here?*

"What the donkle are you doing here in our camp?" Gaffer growled as he and his brother stumbled toward Ginch. "Who the dingle-dangle are you?"

"Me? I'm-a Antonio Chicolini. The boss, she send-a me," he said, pointing at the red cap atop his hat.

"One of us, eh?" the spriggan said, stalking over and bending down low to look Ginch in the eyes. "Roight—'Oo exactly is our boss then?"

"The Doochess of-a the Sighs. About so tall, got-a the scar on-a the cheek, yells all of the time. Anyway, she tell-a me to tell-a you that the hunt, it run-a long so— 'Ey! You got-a the sproot in there with-a the bambino!"

"Yeah, we caught her trying to—"

"Has she got-a the owl on the back?"

"Yeah! How do you—"

"The boss, she look-a for that sproot! And you catch-a her! Oh, the boss, she's-a gonna give-a you the big, big bonus for this!"

The red-capped gang all looked pleased by the news. "I tell you ve get ein bonus!" Wolfgang said proudly.

"Yeah, you definitely get-a the bonus," Ginch said. He gave his deck a quick shuffle. "So now, since we got-a the time, maybe we see who gets-a the . . . *extra bonus*? Who's-a in, eh?"

There was general agreement that this was an excellent idea, so Ginch gathered them over by the fire and dealt a hand. Shade turned away and squinted into the darkness. *If Ginch is here,* she reasoned, *then somewhere around here must be the*—"Professor!" she whispered when the dandelion-headed pixie sprang on his grasshopper legs silently out of the dark and landed in front of her, grinning, with his arms held out to either side. "What are you two doing here?"

The Professor held a finger to his lips to silence her, then crouched down by the crying baby and stuck his tongue out and puffed out his cheeks. The baby stopped crying and looked at him. He did it again, and the baby giggled. The pixie reached in, gave him a tickle under the chin that made him coo, then reached deep into a pants pocket and pulled out a big ring covered in what looked like a hundred keys. He chose one, tried it in the padlock, and then tried another when that one failed.

Key after key the Professor tried, pausing occasionally to make a face or tickle the baby, while Shade kept glancing nervously toward the campfire, fearful that one of the Sluagh gang would look their way. Fortunately, Ginch kept the gang's attention by telling stories and jokes and making sure that each player won a hand or two early on so that they focused all the more on the game as Ginch started to win more and more.

Eventually, after many, many tries and many, many card games, the lock snapped open. The Professor gave Shade a thumbs-up and silently lifted the top of the cage. Shade fluttered out. When she landed, the

Professor grabbed her arm and tried to run, but Shade didn't budge. "We can't go yet!"

The Professor nodded and tried to go again but was again stopped by Shade. "We have to save the baby! We can't just leave him here."

The two looked over toward the card game to see a troubled looking Ginch looking back. He made a slight shooing motion with his hand in their direction.

"The baby," Shade mouthed at him.

Ginch frowned and repeated his shooing motion.

"Vat are you doink?" the wulver asked. "Vit your hand—vat are you doink?"

"Oh, this?" Ginch shook his hand more vigorously. "I just got-a the rummiatism. I give-a it a shake or two to work-a out the—"

A couple cards, both of them the Ace of Hearts, flew out of his sleeve and hit the spriggan on his long, crooked nose. All the gang members stood up and surrounded Ginch.

"That's-a funny!" Ginch shook his head. "I wonder how-a those cards accidentally get in-a my sleeve . . ."

The spriggan reached down, grabbed the back of Ginch's coat, and hauled him up to eye level. The little brownie's legs dangled several feet above the ground.

"You can think about it while we accidentally peel you like a grape," one of the goblins growled, pulling out a dagger.

"Or while oi accidently eat ya for me bedtoim snack," the spriggan said, drool running down his chin.

Ginch gulped and, for the first time since Shade met him, seemed much like the Professor for a moment: completely speechless.

In which Shade sees the Professor
perform and gets menaced by a
mother . . .

As Shade and the Professor watched in horror, the
spriggan lowered Ginch to the ground and held
him in place with his arms pinned to his sides.
The hyena-headed goblin stepped forward and placed
the tip of his knife against Ginch's throat. "Now let's
see . . . Where should we start?"

Shade grabbed the Professor by his lapels. "We've
got to do something! They'll kill him!"

But what? Shade wondered. *I can't pull the owl trick on them—they're too big. Maybe we could distract them but—*

"H-h-h-hey!" a sweet, high voice shouted. The Professor bounded over to the campfire. "St-st-stop!"

"The Professor can talk?" Shade whispered.

"You can-a talk?" Ginch gasped, as the Professor landed on nimble feet next to him. "Since when can-a you talk?"

"S-s-since always. B-b-b—"

"Ve haf regular feast, mein friends!" the wulver laughed, taking a step toward the Professor. "Maybe ve eat pixie first unt haf brownie for dessert, ja?"

"How-how-how 'bout s-some e-e-enter-t-t-tainment f-first," the Professor stuttered. He began to dance a lively jig, skipping and hopping about, yet with a wonderful grace to it, the sort of gracefulness that can only be achieved if you have legs like a cricket and knees that bend backwards. If you've ever seen someone with legs like these dance, then you know exactly what I'm talking about. If you haven't, I highly recommend you widen your circle of friends a bit and expose yourself to more diverse people and experiences.

The fairy gang exchanged puzzled and amused looks before moving to capture the pixie. He danced nimbly out of their way, opened his mouth, and, after a few stutters, began to sing in a beautiful, lilting manner:

Hey nonny hey,
Come and play, come and play.
Hey nonny hey,
Do as I say.

Hey nonny ho,
Time to go, time to go.
Hey nonny ho,
Know that it's so.

Hey, nonny, hee,
Come with me, come with me.
Hey, nonny, hee,
Let's go to the sea.

Shade was mesmerized by the pixie's singing. *What a beautiful voice!* She smiled serenely. *I wish I could listen to it always! And yes, it is time to go play by the sea! Hey nonny ho, let's go!*

Shade smiled at the gang and Ginch, all of whom—goblin twins, wulver, spriggan, and Ginch—smiled back, looking just as peaceful and pleased as she. The Professor spun around and pranced away from the fire into the darkness of the night, repeating his song as he went. *Oh good!* Shade thought when she saw everyone else was also skipping along after the Professor. *We can all go play by the sea together! What fun!*

The Professor sang and skipped, trilled and twirled, piped and pranced, crooned and cavorted, until they reached the edge of a high cliff overlooking the sea. *Well, this will be a lovely place to play!* Shade nodded appreciatively at the lush grass and the lofty view.

Shade's desire to play, however, came to an abrupt end as the Professor suddenly stopped singing and dancing. He faced them all with his back to the ocean, the cliff edge less than a foot behind him, then stuck out his tongue and blew a raspberry while thumbing his nose.

The Sluagh gang growled, to which the Professor responded by turning around and wiggling his behind at them. With cries of rage and unrepeatable insults, they charged at the pixie. Just before they could grab him, the Professor launched himself over their heads. Speeding past him, the wulver flew over the cliff's edge, followed by hyena-headed Laffer who had almost stopped short when his twin Gaffer slammed into him, sending them both tumbling painfully down the rocky cliffs to join their lupine companion in the dark waters below.

Only the spriggan halted in time, but that did him little good when the Professor sprang back and kicked him with both feet in back of the knees. Struggs flailed wildly as he tipped over the edge and landed on a jagged patch of rocks. There was a popping sound and the spriggan went sailing erratically through the air and then eventually out over the water with green, foul-smelling gas shooting out a hole in his side with a loud, continuous, farty *BRAAAAP!* When he was nearly out of view, the sound finally ended. A moment later, there was a quiet little splash.

Shade and Ginch turned to see the Professor panting, grinning with the tip of his tongue sticking out. Ginch threw his arms around him. "Ha-ha! You save-a us!" He stopped hugging and held the pixie at arms' length. "'Ey, how come in all of the years you my partner you no tell-a me you can-a talk?"

The Professor shrugged. "Y-you n-n-never asked."

Shade had stood back this whole time watching the two but couldn't contain herself any longer. She threw her arms around them both. "I'm so happy to see you! After all the mean things I said to you, you still came and freed me!"

"We figure we owe you," Ginch replied. "Plus, the Professor, he take-a the shine to you. Me, I no mind-a you company too much."

"Thanks," Shade smirked. "I guess I don't mind your company too much either."

The Professor whistled and pointed back toward the campfire. "B-b-baby?"

"The baby!" The three sprinted back to the campsite to find the baby curled up asleep in a corner of the cage. Together the three slowly tipped the cage over.

"Okay, we have to carry him back to his house," Shade said. "Professor, you carry the end with the head; Ginch, you take the middle; I'll get the feet."

Ginch made a face and shook his head. "Oh no. I no take-a the stinky part."

Shade and the Professor put their hands under their respective ends of the baby. "It's a baby—every part of it's the stinky part. Just grab and lift."

Carefully the fairies lifted the baby over their heads, carried him back to his cottage, and placed him in front of the door. Ginch raised his hand to knock, but Shade stopped him. "Wait! We can't just knock on the door."

"Why not?"

"The parents are humans. They won't be able to see us—they'll just find their baby on the ground. Plus there's a changeling, which the parents will be able to see, that looks just like their son in the baby's bed."

Ginch scratched his head. "Maybe if we tell-a the changeling-a-ding that the jig's-a up, he'll skee-deedle."

The Professor nodded vigorously then dragged the two over to the window of the baby's room.

"There's no way that he'll—" Shade began to object but was cut off by the Professor grabbing her around the legs and tossing her up and into the open window. She just managed to open her wings in time to keep from crashing on the floor. Instead, she was knocked to the floor when Ginch's body flew through the window right after her.

Ginch got up, dusted himself off, and walked to the crib. He pointed a finger in the cooing baby's face. "All right! Hit-a the bricks, fatcha-coota-matchca, baby-face!"

The "baby" reached up, grabbed him by the ears, and slammed his head against the side of the crib. Ginch staggered back as the changeling stood up, grabbed his cigar from the nightstand, and took a puff while leaning on the side of the crib. "Aw yeah?" he said in his gruff, gravelly voice. "Who's gonna make me, huh?"

In the next room, Shade heard a knock and then someone open a door. A woman's voice cried out, "Me baby! What's me baby doin' out here?"

"We're going to make you, slug slime!" Shade said. "You better jump out that window before that mother comes in and catches you!"

"Aw, horse apples!" the changeling sneered as he chomped on his cigar. "I can out baby any stoopid baby! When I'm done wit' my act, she'll chuck her own brat out dat windah!"

The Professor vaulted through the window and landed as silently and gracefully as a cat. In one hand he held a tin cup with something rattling inside. He pointed at the changeling with his free hand and then hooked a thumb over his shoulder.

"Oh, you wanna piece a me too, pixie-pants!" The changeling puffed his cigar and balled up his fists. "Awright, come get some, youse mooks! I'll pound tha lot a yas!"

The Professor held up the tin cup and rattled its contents. With a wicked grin on his face, he flung it at the changeling—an iron nail. The changeling shrieked and wailed and swore as it struck him in the chest, causing his flesh to sizzle and blister. The changeling leapt out the window, swearing revenge and just plain swearing.

"You get-a the nail from the barn?" Ginch asked. The Professor nodded. "Ha-ha! That's-a good! Okay, we got-a—"

Just then the doorknob started to turn. "Okay, as long as we stay out of the humans' way, they shouldn't see us or hear us," Shade whispered. "So up against the wall, and we'll get out of here with the baby's parents none the wiser."

The door opened and there, lantern light streaming in around her, stood a fair-skinned blond woman wearing a brown peasant dress. One hand clutched her infant to her chest; the other brandished an iron fireplace poker. "Roight, ye wee folk! Which one o' ye's been muckin' about wi' me little Bran?"

"You can see us?" Shade gasped.

"'Course oi can see ye," she snorted. "Drank a glass o' milk backwards after refusin' to do me chores first thing on Saint Bartleby the Unwillin's Day when oi were ten. Been able to see ye wee boogers ever since. Now what ye be doin' here?"

"The goblins, they take-a the bambino!" Ginch said, raising his hands above his head. "We bring-a him back and chase-a off the changeling-a-ding they put-a in-a the crib. He scream-a the bloody murder, he do-a! You gotta believe-a us!"

"Well, maybe oi believe ye and maybe oi don't, but ye better believe oi want ye to clear out o' me house. Ye can sleep in the bairn for the noight if ye want but oi'll give ye a taste o' dis poker if ye're still 'round when mornin' come. Now sod off, the lot o' ye!"

Needing no second warning, the three scrambled out the window, with only the Professor pausing to blow the baby a kiss on the way.

"And take yer bloody cigar with ye!" the mother called, chucking it out the window.

20

In which expectations are unsuccessfully managed and then dashed . . .

"I know we're going to find the library today. I just know it!" Shade declared cheerfully as they set out immediately at daybreak, partly due to eagerness and partly due to a recently acquired fear of mothers with iron pokers. "I wonder if they'll have copies of all the books we used to have: *The Hasty and Increasingly Poor Choices of Romulus and Julianna* by

William Shudderpike. And Lee the Harper's *To Murder an Insulting Finch*! And—"

"'Ey, little Sprootshade . . ." Ginch tapped her lightly on the shoulder.

"Maybe they need a copy of Radishbottom's book. I could donate mine along with my corrections if they let me stay there. My stuff could be in a library!" Shade's eyes grew wide. "I wonder how many books they've got. Hundreds? Thousands? Hundreds of thousands?"

FWEEET! The Professor's shrill whistle startled Shade enough to quiet her for a second. The pixie pointed at Ginch.

"Oh! Sorry!" Shade smiled, continuing to walk. "Were you saying something?"

"Yeah." Ginch looked at the ground. "I just wonder . . . you know . . . what if-a the library, uh . . . it's-a no there no more?"

"What?" Shade halted abruptly, causing the Professor to bump into her.

"I mean, we have-a the big, big war and—"

Shade closed her eyes and shook her head. *Why is he talking rot?* she wondered. "It *has* to be there.

"I . . . I just no want-a you to get-a you hopes up too high." Ginch jammed his hands in his pockets and faced the sea.

Shade's face grew hot. She felt betrayed. "The library *will* be there. They *will* let me in. Come on, we're wasting time!"

Shade stomped off, furious at Ginch for trying to ruin things. Ginch and the Professor exchanged a worried look, then hurried after her. For a long time, the three traveled in silence, hiking along the coast, high atop cliffs and down along pebbly shores. The sun shone brightly in a cloudless, powder blue sky, its light shimmering on the surface of the brilliant turquoise sea as brisk breezes blew inland.

Shade's anger with Ginch had abated somewhat when they stopped for a rest and brief morning snack, but she was still annoyed with him. Ginch took his handful of berries and said, "You two relax. I take-a the peek from the hill up-a there."

As he walked away, the Professor took from various pockets a notebook, a quill, and an inkwell and began to write furiously. "What are you doing?" Shade asked.

The Professor tore out the page and handed it to Shade. It read: *Don't be mad. He just doesn't want you to be disappointed.*

Shade snorted. "What does he know about disappointment? Everything's either a game or a joke to him."

The Professor scribbled another note: *That's what he wants everyone to think. His home was destroyed in one of the wars.*

Shade's brow furrowed. "But I thought he was just a lazy crook."

He is, the Professor wrote. *But he loved that cottage and the family in it. He's never really gotten over the loss.*

Shade looked over at the figure standing at the top of the hill, slightly slouched with his hands jammed in his pockets. Up to this point, Shade had always thought his threadbare, too-tight clothes looked comical; at this moment, however, they struck her as extremely sad. "I had no idea," she said quietly. "Why didn't you tell me before? I mean, you *can* speak. I've heard you."

The words always get stuck in my throat, he wrote. *For me, it's easier to speak without words.*

"Then why haven't you written us any notes before?"

Ginch is the best friend I've ever had. I don't need words, written or spoken, for him to understand me.

"Sprootshade! 'Ey, little Sprootshade!" Ginch called, rushing down the hill. The Professor stuffed the writing implements into a pocket and crammed the written notes into his mouth and chewed. "The Marble Cliffs! I see-a the Marble Cliffs!"

There from the top of the hill, Shade saw them: gleaming white cliffs veined with glittering gold and silver rising high above the brilliant blue sea that lapped at its base. She had never seen anything so majestic, so awe-inspiring. She squinted at the cliffs, searching for some glimpse of the library Baba Ingas had told her about. There was no sign of any buildings; the only thing of note was a massive tree that loomed large there. *Maybe it's behind the tree?* Shade wondered.

Or under it or further along the cliffs? But it's up there. I know it's up there.

Having their long-sought-after goal in sight, the three resumed their trek with the manic energy that comes when a dream seems about to come true. The cold winds that had chilled before now invigorated. Rather than be wearied by the ever-steepening slope as they followed the cliffs, they felt heartened and challenged by it.

Shade looked at Ginch and the Professor, who followed red-faced and smiling right behind her. They looked just as excited as she was to be nearing the library, yet she knew that neither of them had really wanted to go there. *They're not excited because this is what they want,* she realized. *They're excited because this is what I want.*

Shade tried to tell herself that it was the cold breeze that made tears well up in her eyes at that moment, but I'm the narrator of this story, and you are a very astute Reader; so we know better, don't we?

"Ginch? Professor?" Shade said as she wiped her

eyes. "I never would have made it here if it weren't for the two of you—"

Ginch waved a hand dismissively. "Aw, we no help-a much—you would-a managed just-a fine on you own."

"That's not true. I wouldn't have even made it past Gypsum-upon-Swathmud without you."

"Neither would-a we," Ginch chuckled. The Professor nodded, drew his thumb across his neck, stuck out his tongue, and rolled his eyes back in his head.

"Look, what I'm trying to say is . . ." Shade looked down at her feet. "Thank you."

The ground leveled off as they reached the summit of the Marble Cliffs. "Without you, I never would have made it to the li . . ."

Shade trailed off and gawped, speechless, at what she saw at the apex of the Marble Cliffs.

Or, rather, what she didn't see.

"You *really* no need-a to thank us, little Sprootshade," Ginch said gently. "The library—it's-a no here."

In which the description of the
chapter is not at all helpful . . .

W e've all been disappointed many times in our
lives, and so we all know that the biggest dis-
appointments come when we have great expectations that are not met. I believe a fellow named
Dickens wrote a book all about this, although the
name of it escapes me at the moment. Now, to better
understand Shade's disappointment at this point in

our tale, I'd like you to think about the time that your beloved Aunt Esther—the one who travels to all sorts of exotic locales—gave you those two wrapped presents, which looked exactly the right size to be the Balinese dueling daggers and shrunken head that you had been hounding her about for years, that turned out to be a knitting kit and a souvenir hockey puck from Muncie, Indiana. Now take how you felt as you held in your hands a pair of knitting needles and a puck with "Muncie Flyers" inscribed on the side and multiply it by about a thousand, and you'd come close to feeling the disappointment that Shade felt on top of that cliff that day as she found nothing resembling a library whatsoever.

This is not to say that the clifftop was completely barren. The tree that they had seen from below was there: an ancient, gnarled oak that towered above them, as wide around as a church, its rough, gray-brown bark overgrown with moss, lichen, and ivy, and its fiery autumnal leaves all but blotting out the sky above them and rustling amongst the patchy grass and twisted, exposed roots beneath their feet. It was the biggest tree any of them had ever seen, and one all but guaranteed to inspire awe in the heart of any who saw it.

"All there is is this stupid, useless tree!" Shade spat as she whirled about, searching the top of the cliff. "Where's the dingle-dangle library? Ingas said it would be here!"

"Maybe . . . maybe we get-a the wrong part of the cliffs?" Ginch suggested hopefully.

Shade gestured around her. "This is the highest point of the cliffs."

The professor whistled, took a pair of binoculars out of his coat, and pointed up.

"There's nothing to see!" Shade cried as she collapsed on the ground. "We can see the rest of the cliffs from here, and *there is no library.*"

The Professor, who was having trouble finding a good foothold, rounded the trunk until he was out of sight. Ginch sat down next to Shade and put his arm around her.

"You were right about not getting my hopes up," Shade sniffed. "I wanted this so badly. And now, after all that I've been through—"

"*We*," Ginch said. "All *we* have-a been through. Together. And don't-a give up yet, little Sprootshade. Maybe the Ingas, she get-a the wrong place? Yeah, that's-a it! She get-a the wrong place, so we—"

"Just stop, Ginch. Please." Shade sighed. "It's over. There is no library. If there ever was, it's gone."

The Professor whistled from the other side of the tree.

"Yeah, that's-a the good bird impression, Professor," Ginch called. "So like-a I say, we go to Gypsum, we go to Bilgewater, we go to Thunder-ten-Tronckh—we go all over the place, and we find-a out where this library is and—"

The Professor whistled again, higher and sharper than before.

"I no know-a that one, Professor! Is it the double-roofled hoop-pooh? 'Cause I never even hear of that bird and think-a I just make it up!" Ginch shouted.

"So we find-a the place, and if we no find-a it, then we get-a you the books—so many books—"

The Professor rounded the corner of the tree, eyes glaring and teeth bared. He gave a sharp whistle, grabbed them by their collars, and dragged them around the tree, ignoring their objections, exclamations (mostly rude), and struggling, until he brought them to the side of the tree that directly faced the ocean, at which point he tossed them both to the ground.

Shade stopped yelling when she finally looked at the part of the tree that the Professor had been emphatically pointing at during her tirade. It was a door! An easy-to-miss door, what with it being covered with the same lichen- and moss-covered bark as the rest of the tree, its outline barely distinguishable from the natural cracks and patterns of the trunk, and its knob looking like little more than the sort of knot that routinely forms on old English oaks, but a door nonetheless. Shade's pulse quickened.

Ginch tapped her on the shoulder. "'Ey, Sprootshade, you no think-a . . ."

Shade nodded. "It has to be."

They stood there silent for a moment, the only sounds being the rattling of leaves, the splashing of distant waves, and the far-off cries of seagulls.

"So, what you think-a we do to get-a in?" Ginch asked.

"Maybe a password?" Shade said. "Secret doors in books usually require a password."

"Swordfish!" Ginch shouted.

"What?"

"Swordfish. The password, it's-a always 'swordfish.'" Ginch looked at the door, which didn't budge. "Except when it isn't."

"Or maybe we have to answer a riddle," Shade mused. "Yeah, just like in Revel's *There and Back Again and Then Back There and Part Way Back Again Before Doubling Back for the Thing They Forgot and Then All the Way Back for Real This Time!*"

The Professor rolled his eyes, grabbed the knob, twisted, and opened the door inwards. He motioned for Shade and Ginch to go in then, when they just stood there dumbfounded, shoved them both inside.

I know—I was hoping for some sort of riddle or password or grim, spectral guardian myself. We'll just have to add it to our lists of grievances with this story and take what we are given, I suppose.

On the other side of the door was a vast, circular hall filled with long wooden tables and blocks of study nooks at which sat a score of fairies—a number of elves, several trows, a pair of dwarves hunched over a map, a few goblins, some gnomes whispering to one another, a dozing hobgoblin, and an old human in long gray robes and a funny hat poring over books about rings. The walls were covered in books—shelves and shelves crammed with books, more books than Shade had ever believed could exist, in all the colors of the rainbow and of every size from the thinnest pamphlet to tomes so big that Shade doubted she could lift them.

Shade gave a little squeal and raced across the polished wood floor that showed thousands of years' worth of tree rings to get to the nearest bookshelf. There—*Romulus and Julianna*! And there—*Hagan*

Finnegan! But next to them were books by the same authors she had never seen before: *The Adventures of Lying Thom Woodcutter; A Cornish Pixie in King Pendragon's Court; A Late-Autumn Afternoon's Woolgathering; Julius and the Terrible, Horrible, No Good, Very Bad Day in the Senate*; and at least thirty others! And next to them were books by completely new authors she had never even heard of: *The Laughable Optimism of Dr. Pangloss; Winston the Bugbear; The Man Who Was Wednesday; The Bobcat, the Prestidigitator, and the Armoire;* and so, so many more.

Shade felt dizzy with glee. She wanted to gorge herself on the books in front of her. And then . . . then she wanted to read every book in the next case and then the next and then the next.

"Oh my gosh," Shade whispered, turning to see Ginch and the Professor's happy smiles. "Ginch, how many books do you think they have here?"

"What? You mean on-a this wall, on-a this floor, or in-a the whole place?" Ginch pointed up. Somehow, in her amazement, Shade hadn't noticed the walkway that spiraled from the ground floor up and up and up inside the tree and that the walls, as far as the eye could see, were covered in books! "Depending on what-a you ask, I say either 'a lot,' 'a whole lot,' or 'too many to say.'"

Shade's head swam. After growing up reading the same seventy-four books over and over again, the idea of being surrounded by more books than she could ever hope to read in her lifetime was exhilarating but at the same time slightly intimidating and oddly sad, much like when you are given the chance to eat as much chocolate cake as you like and realize that eating even half of it would give you a tummy ache and finishing the whole thing would just be impossible. But putting that aside, chocolate cake is chocolate cake and books are books and having as much as you could ever want of either is a wonderful thing.

"I need to spend the rest of my life here!" Shade looked at the Professor and Ginch with wide, hopeful eyes. "How do you think I go about doing that?"

The Professor and Ginch scratched their heads and

looked around. The Professor gave a quick whistle—to which almost every person in the hall responded with a testy "Shhhh!"—and pointed to the middle of the hall. There in the center of the concentric circles was a large wooden desk with a high-backed leather chair behind it. Seated in that chair was a black cat wearing a loose cream-colored shirt, unbuttoned brown vest, and rectangular spectacles.

"You should talk-a to the kitty-guy," Ginch said decisively.

"How do you know?"

"Because he's got-a the big, big chair. The person with the biggest chair is-a usually the one to talk-a to."

Shade thought for a second. "That actually makes some sense."

"Everything I say make-a the perfect sense! Now you go ask-a the kitty to give-a you the job."

22

In which Shade talks to people
with big, big chairs . . .

S hade walked as quietly as she could—she felt
that her boots were far too loud for the echoey
hall—up to the large desk, which was piled
with books, most of which appeared to be damaged—
torn and missing covers, loose pages, split spines, etc.
In the midst of them, the bespectacled cat hunched
over a ledger in which he wrote slowly and methodi-
cally with a quill pen.

"Excuse me," Shade whispered, "but I—"

Without looking up, the cat held up a single claw on his non-writing paw. "One moment, if you please," he said. He spoke with a slight accent, similar to the wulvers Shade had encountered, but nowhere near as thick. "Vait—I am being very busy vith cataloging books for repairs. I vill call Caxton, our library's dogsbody. Caxton!" the cat called. A chorus of shushing rose from the study tables. "Caxton!"

"Sod off, mouse-breaf!" a deep, growly voice shouted from the floor above, again eliciting an annoyed shushing.

"Caxton, come. Ve have new scholars!"

There was a moment of silence followed by a resigned "A'roight, oi'll come down then, Johannes. Oi could use a bit of a break from Dewey's bloody reorganoizin'."

As feet clomped from above, the Professor and Ginch wandered over to join Shade. The cat rubbed his paws together. "So, how may I help you and your . . ." the cat cast a skeptical glance at Ginch, who was whistling and rocking back and forth with his hands jammed in his pockets, and the Professor, who grinned his silly, tongue-tipped grin, "fellow scholars?"

"Well . . . I was hoping . . ." Shade stopped, afraid to speak. It can be a very scary thing to tell someone about your dreams, even more so when telling them might actually make those dreams come true. But Shade found her courage and blurted out, "I was really hoping I could stay here. Like work and live here or something. I don't know. I just . . . I just really want to spend the rest of my life surrounded by books."

The cat frowned thoughtfully. "Vell, I don't know. Ve're pretty vell staffed at the moment, and ve usually employ scholars . . ."

"She's-a the scholar!" Ginch piped up. The Professor nodded. "She's-a the great, great scholar! Sprootshade, show him you book and-a you notes."

Shade took off her backpack and pulled out her copy of Radishbottom's book and her notebook. "I've had this Radishbottom book all my life," she explained. "I'd be happy to . . . donate it to the library as well as this book of corrections and annotations I've been working on—I'm afraid there are some pretty major errors and omissions in it—if you took me on," Shade said, hoping she didn't sound as desperate as she felt.

The cat opened his mouth to speak but was interrupted by a fairy with a white and brown bulldog's head topped with a black bowler hat cocked rakishly askew, an unlit cigar jutting from the corner of his mouth. "A'roight, what ya be needin' then, fleabag?" he growled, snapping shut a silver pocket watch before tucking it into the pocket of his black, pinstriped vest.

The cat chuckled. "Don't mind him. He's not as gruff as he seems."

"Yes, oi am," the dog man grumbled.

"Always vith the jokes!" the cat laughed. "Caxton, please to be taking these three to the head librarians, ja? They vish to discuss employment."

As they spiraled up through the floors of the library, Shade reached out her hand and touched the books lining the walls. Feeling the leather, cloth, and paper under her fingers reassured her that they were real.

They wound their way up to the tenth floor, and Caxton led them to a round-topped doorway. The open door revealed a large office or study with a floor-to-ceiling picture window that overlooked the glittering sea. The walls flanking the window were covered in paintings of fairies of all types reading or writing. Two immense desks (behind which were leather chairs so large they put Johannes's to shame) faced each other from opposite sides of the room, which was cluttered with books, scrolls, statues, globes, skeletons, telescopes, microscopes, beakers, and other odds and ends. A map lay unfurled on top of one of the desks, over which stood a gorgeous woman in a long, elegant gown, every inch of her as smooth and pure white as if she were made of alabaster. Next to her, wearing a white ruffled shirt, crimson waistcoat, and shiny blue jacket and knee-pants (an outfit that would have made Chauncey the Gentletroll swoon) and sipping coffee from a china cup stood a pointy-eared, bat-winged fairy, his face like that of a monkey's only with a slightly longer snout, his skin dark gray and rough, horns poking out from under the curly, shoulder-length white wig he wore atop his head.

"Oui, mon petit chou," the gargoyle said as they entered, pointing at the map with his free hand, "but ze middle of ze land—"

"Oi, bosses!" Caxton interrupted. The gargoyle and the white lady looked up from the map. Shade clutched her copy of Radishbottom's book, its cover facing out, as if to ward off rejection and prove her worth by displaying the last remnant of her beloved library. "We've got—"

"Mon dieu!" the gargoyle exclaimed, his eyes wide. "Émilie, is zat—"

"Oui!" the white woman replied. "It is!"

The gargoyle set his coffee mug down with a clatter.

"Croiky! The boss put down 'is coffee!" Caxton gasped. He dashed out of the room and shouted, "Johannes! Johannes! The boss put down 'is coffee!"

Shade looked to the equally puzzled Ginch and Professor as the gargoyle and the alabaster woman rushed toward them.

In which the wonders of the library
are revealed . . .

My book! Shade thought as the head librarians neared, and the gargoyle reached out his hand. *It must be rare. That would make it a valuable acquisition! They'll have to let me stay if—*

But instead of grabbing the book, the gargoyle instead grasped the Professor's hand and shook it vigorously. "Professor! It is such ze honor to 'ave you 'ere at our library!"

"Wait a minote! You know-a the Professor?" Ginch asked.

"Mais oui! Well, we've never met, but I've read many of Professor Pinky's treatises and monographs on intraspatial studies and pure, applied, and 'istorical pocketry. In fact . . ." The gargoyle reached into his jacket and pulled out a steaming pot of coffee. He grinned, and his eyes twinkled merrily. "In case I ever find myself with an empty cup out in ze stacks!"

"You're really a professor?" Shade asked.

The Professor nodded and pulled from a pocket the book *Pick a Pocket: A History of Stylistic and Functional Design in the Field of Applied Pocketry* and showed her the back cover, which featured a sketch of the Professor (tongue-tip protruding from a silly grin) under which was written, "Lucius Theodosius 'Lucky' Pinky, University of Streüseldorff Professor of Intraspatial Studies and Distinguished Chair of Pocketry."

"See, I tell-a you he look-a like a professor," Ginch said.

"My dear Professor Pinky," the white woman said in

a voice as smooth as her polished marble skin, "allow me to formally welcome you and your associates to our library. May I introduce my partner and cohead of the library, Monsieur François Marie?"

The gargoyle gave the Professor a short bow that the Professor returned. "And may I in turn introduce you to ze overly modest and true 'ead of zis library, Madame Émilie Tonnelier, la Dame Blanche."

The alabaster woman curtsied, and so did the Professor. She then walked, so elegantly that it seemed more like she glided, over to Shade and Ginch and extended a hand to each one. It was smooth, hard, and cold. "We know the illustrious Professor Pinky, but as for you—"

"I'm-a the Ginch," Ginch broke in. "Rigoletto Ginch. And she's-a the Sprootshade."

Shade elbowed him hard with her free arm. "Actually, it's just Shade."

"An absolute pleasure," François declared. "Now, Professor, 'ow might we be of service? We are prepared to put our every resource at your disposal. No doubt you 'ave come to research somezing of great—"

The Professor waved his hands and whistled *Twee-Twoo!* then pointed to Shade.

With all eyes on her, Shade cleared her throat and spoke. "Actually, we're here because of me. I've come a long way, from Pleasant Hollow in the Merry Forest."

"Such dedication! Such a journey!" Émilie declared.

"And all the way from ze very center of ze kingdom out to our little cliffs by ze sea," François said, arching an eyebrow at Émilie. "Is zis Pleasant 'Ollow your 'ome?"

"It was until my house burned down, and all my books with it. Except this one." Shade held out the Radishbottom book to Émilie, who took it.

"Oh, look, François! Radishbottom's *Traveling in the Greater Kingdom*."

"Which edition?"

"Em . . . Second."

"There's more than one edition?" Shade asked.

"Four," François replied.

"Oui," Émilie concurred. "He made additions and corrections in each subsequent edition."

"Oh." Shade's efforts suddenly felt pointless; her book, worthless. "I don't suppose you'd, um, want the book or these notes and corrections I've been making?"

"We 'ave several copies of ze book," François explained as he waved it away. He did, however, take her notebook in his rough granite hands. "'Owever, I would be delighted to see your original work. Now, may I presume to ask what exactly 'as brought you so far, wiz such illustrious companions, to our little sanctuary of learning?"

"I . . . Well, you see . . . I'd like to work here. To live here. To be with books for the rest of my life."

Émilie and François looked to each other. He reached over, picked up his coffee cup from the desk, and took a sip. They said nothing.

"Little Sprootshade," Ginch jumped in, "books she knows-a the backwards and-a the forwards and-a the sideways! Nobody know or love-a the books like she do!"

The Professor nodded then raised his left hand and put his right over his heart.

"Please, if it's at all possible, it would mean so, so

much to me," Shade said. "I'll do anything here. I could—"

Émilie placed a cold stone hand on her shoulder. "François and I will consider your very generous offer and discuss it in due course. For now, please permit us to give you a tour of our little tree of knowledge."

"Yeah, about that," Shade said as she followed the elegant alabaster woman and coffee-sipping gargoyle out of their office. "Why is your library disguised as a tree? At first, I thought there wasn't even a library here."

"In ze last war," François explained, "'Eremod, ze Sluagh leader, decided zat ze wisdom found in books was ze most dangerous weapon in ze world—"

"And he was right," Émilie added.

"True, *mon cher*. Very true." François winked at Émilie and took a sip of coffee before continuing. "So 'Eremod sends 'is brutes out to burn ze libraries. Ze other two fall but we, we find out in time and, with ze 'elp of wizards and scholars who understand 'ow important places like zis are, 'ide ourselves by becoming a tree because knowledge's roots run deep, it's branches fill ze world, and all live in its benevolent shadow!"

"Plus, I always wanted to live in a metaphor, and this is a rather lovely one," Émilie said, putting her hand on François's arm.

At that moment, a balding, bespectacled brownie with a neatly trimmed beard rushed up. Like Ginch, he was dressed head-to-toe in chocolate brown, but unlike Ginch, this one's three-piece suit was in excellent shape and fit him perfectly, and he wore a precisely tied bowtie that bobbed up and down as he spoke. "I've got it this time!" he cried, his eyes wide with excitement as he waved a sheaf of papers. "Ha-ha! Yes! The perfect organizational system, at last!"

"Our 'ead of general collections, Monsieur Dewey," François explained.

Dewey gave Shade and company a curt nod. "We shall organize *alphabetically* by the fifth word on the eighty-ninth page of every book! It's perfect!"

"But what if the book doesn't have eighty-nine—" Shade began to ask, but the brownie was already gone, laughing and kicking up his heels as he went. She turned to François and Émilie. "That system makes no sense."

François sipped reflectively. "Oh, few of 'is systems do. Émilie, remember when 'e organized zem by weight?"

The white lady smiled. "Or when he arranged them by color?"

"Oh, zat *was* lovely! Ze 'ole library looked like a great rainbow!" The gargoyle chuckled. "'E's quite mad, you know. But 'e takes wonderful care of ze books. And I 'ave faith—'e *will* find ze perfect system someday."

"But if he's constantly reorganizing the books in weird ways, how does anyone find anything?" Shade asked.

The gargoyle's eyes twinkled. "Follow, if you please! Follow!"

The five circled down to the ground floor with François in the lead. Once there, he headed over to a large wooden cabinet filled with tiny drawers, each one labeled with a range of letters, from "A-Ac" in the upper left corner all the way to "Zu-Zz" in the lower right. "Wizin zis cabinet, we 'ave cards zat catalog every book, every scroll, every document, and every artifact wizin zese walls by author, title, and subject, all arranged alphabetically."

"That's really impressive," Shade agreed, "but how does this help anyone find anything if Dewey's constantly donkling with where everything goes?"

"Allow us to demonstrate," Émilie answered. "François, would you be a dear and look up Rabin's *Birds of North Elfame*?"

"D'accord!" François opened one of the drawers, riffled through a series of cards until finally stopping on one. This card he pulled out gently and gave it a little toss. Once out of his fingers, the card folded itself into a bird, gave a papery chirp, and fluttered up to the third floor. "The cards will find the books wherever they may be and wait next to them until they are collected, at which point they will come back and refile themselves."

Shade's heartbeat quickened. *If every book in the library is listed in there,* Shade thought, *I can find out in seconds if . . .*

François smiled knowingly at her, his face, in spite of being a gargoyle's, was the very picture of kindness. "Zere is some special book zat you wish to see, oui?"

"Yes."

Émilie placed a smooth hand on her shoulder. "By all means, have a look."

Shade looked nervously at the four faces that smiled at her, then pulled out the drawer labeled "Go-Gu." *Please let it be here! Please let it be here!* she prayed as she searched. At last her fingers paused. They trembled slightly as they gripped and then pulled loose a card. Shade hesitated, fearing that if she released the card, it would somehow disappear forever. Taking a deep breath, she let go, and the card wafted to the ground. Before it landed, however, it twisted itself into a child with butterfly wings and fluttered off, giggling.

Shade followed it as it flew up and up and up, circling the stacks until they were near the very top of the library, never once taking her eyes off the paper sprite for fear of losing it. At last, it lit upon a shelf and leaned against a thin book bound in red leather. Shade wiped her sweaty palms on her jacket before reaching out for the book on the shelf. Once the book was in her hands, the card blew her a little kiss and then dived over the railing and down the center of the library back to the card catalog.

Shade ran her hand across the cover, which was in much better shape than her copy had been, and years and years of treasured memories came flooding back. Her vision slightly blurred, she opened the cover. There on the title page was a picture of a pair of sprites, a mother and father, tucking a little girl sprite into bed, above which were the words *Goodnight, Little Sprite*. Shade turned the page and read:

Goodnight, little sprite,
Time to sleep tight.
Your day of play is done.
It's time to turn out the light.

Shade wiped away the tears brimming in her eyes for fear of them falling onto the book.

"It's-a the kiddie book," Ginch said over her shoulder.

"Yeah," Shade whispered as she paged through it. "My parents read this to me every night when I was little. I can still recite it word for word. It's the first book I ever loved."

And we all know, no matter how many books we come to read and love in life, how special that first beloved book is, don't we, my friend?

"So what would everyone like to see next?" François asked. "Ze map room? Our grimoire collection? Ze ancient scroll—"

"Actually, could I just have a quiet place to sit and read, please?" Shade asked. "It's just that . . ."

"No need to explain," Émilie said, then led her to a sunny room filled with leather couches and high-backed chairs. "I hope this will suffice."

"It's perfect," Shade said, clutching *Good Night, Little Sprite* to her chest, along with another dozen books she had pulled off the shelves along the way.

François gave her a slight bow, then turned to the Professor. "While Mademoiselle Shade avails 'erself of our library's bounty, Madame Tonnelier and I would be honored to speak to you at lengz in our private offices, my most esteemed Professor."

"He no does-a the talk," Ginch said, pointing at the Professor. "Well, no much, anyway."

"The Professor's embarrassment over his stutter is well-reported in academic circles," Émilie acknowledged. "As are his skills at non-verbal communication. Between that and the wealth of paper and ink in our office, I'm sure we'll do just fine. What do you say, Professor?"

The Professor smiled and gave two thumbs up. As the three left, Ginch took out a deck of cards and began to shuffle them. "I think-a I go see the doggy-guy. He look-a like the easy mark. Unless you need-a me?"

Ginch, who wandered off soon after, may as well have asked the question to one of the books stacked next to Shade's chair as she was already lost in a sea of words. First she read *Goodnight, Little Sprite* cover to cover several times, even though she knew every word by heart, then moved on to her favorite passages in

Hagan Finnegan, The Conquests of Queequeg, Meager Expectations, and other old friends. Books that we love truly are our friends, always there to comfort us in times of trouble, revel with us in times of joy, and inspire countless acts of kindness, nobility, and goodwill every day of our lives. When she'd visited with a good number of old friends, she moved on to introducing herself to new, never-before-seen books and the joys contained therein.

For hours she read voraciously, savoring every word, treasuring each page, all but completely forgetting that her dreams of spending the rest of her life like this were still uncertain, their fulfillment resting in the palms of four cold, stony hands.

24

In which Shade faces a moral
dilemma and ends up thoroughly
donkled . . .

Had Shade turned around, she would have seen
blue and black waves playing and purple clouds
drifting lazily above the setting sun as it glowed
on the horizon where the water met the orange and red
twilight sky. Instead she faced the dark, bark-covered
door that had just been shut in her face.

Shade felt a hand on her shoulder. "We come-a back

tomorrow," Ginch said resolutely. "We come-a back tomorrow, and we show them they make-a the big, big mistake, and we get-a you the job. You leave it to me. I'm-a the shrewd negotiator. Why once I—"

"Oh, shut up," Shade sighed, brushing off his hand. Without looking at him or the Professor—for she could not bear their pitying looks—she trudged over to a rock overlooking the sea. She sat down and sulked, her mind going over again and again what had been said to her after hours of lovely reading.

"We're sorry, but we just don't have any need for more workers."

"Zere just is not ze room for more fairies to live 'ere amongst ze books."

"You are, like all book lovers, always welcome to come visit whenever you can."

"Oui! And we 'ope to see you again soon and often!"

For the first time in her very literate life, Shade was at a complete loss for words. She had had no words to respond to Émilie and François as they had crushed her dreams and ushered her out of the library ("We must close up for ze night," they had said); she had no words to express how desolate and angry she felt; she could remember no words from anything she had ever read to comfort her in this, her lowest moment. She felt empty, like the cover of a book whose pages had been ripped out. I won't share with you what Shade thought must be written on the cover, but suffice it to say that it might shock your sweet, delicate Aunt Petunia into an early grave if she were to read it.

Ginch and the Professor sat on either side of her. They said and did nothing for a time. Shade didn't look at either of her friends, instead silently watching the sea ebb and flow far down below. She sniffed and rubbed her eyes. She suddenly felt very, very tired.

The Professor nudged her. When she turned to face him, he grinned—which kind of made her want to slap his pale, silly face—reached into his jacket, and handed her a book. She opened its red leather cover and in the light of the setting sun read, "Goodnight, little sprite, Time to sleep tight."

Shade looked at the Professor in disbelief. "You stole this. You stole this from the library . . . for me."

He shrugged. He was still grinning, but now Shade could see the sadness in it she had overlooked before. She looked back at the book. There it was: *her* book. The one thing she wanted most in the world, and it was hers for the taking. She could have it with her always. She could read it whenever she felt lonely or scared—why, she could read it every night and day no matter what! Maybe, in time, she could find more books and build herself a new collection with *Goodnight, Little Sprite* and Radishbottom's book as its core and find a new home—*Weren't they going to build me a new one back in Pleasant Hollow?* she remembered—and spend the rest of her days surrounded by books that were hers and hers alone, always there at hand whenever she needed them.

Then she remembered what had happened to all her books before. How could she guarantee that this book would be safe when her last copy, through absolutely no fault of her own, was gone forever? Wouldn't it be much safer in the library? And what if there was some other sprite out there—or brownie or pixie or goblin or kobold or what have you—who was desperately looking for this special, special book and who, like her, came a long, long way and endured hardship after hardship to get to this magical place? Did Shade's love—her *need*—for this book really give her the right to deny that fairy the chance to ever read it?

"Oh, pucknernuts!" she groaned. "Professor, I really appreciate what you tried to do here, but . . . I can't keep this. We've got to give it back."

With book in hand, Shade got up to go pound on the library door and return the book.

"Oh, did you think you were going somewhere?" a harsh, unfortunately familiar voice sneered.

Shade's eyes grew wide. "We are so dingled and dangled," she muttered.

"And-a donkled," Ginch replied. "Really, really, donkled."

In which enemies attack and your humble narrator's favorite character reappears (Finally!) . . .

L ady Perchta stood there, gleaming short sword in hand. She was still clad in the bronze and leather armor from her Wild Hunt but no longer wore her helmet. Her silvery hair fluttered in the breeze as she sneered at Shade. Around her, looking battered and bruised and none too friendly, were a wulver, a spriggan, and twin hyena-headed goblins. In the near distance, mounted on their horses and clutching spears, were three members of the Wild Hunt—those with the wolverine, bear, and wolf heads—next to whom stood four large, armor-clad humans, their faces scarred and vicious.

Ginch stepped in front of Shade. "'Ey, you no can-a hurt the little Sprootshade! You're on-a the Wild Hunt and—"

The wolverine-helmed goblin reached into a saddle bag and tossed something that landed with a thud in front of Ginch. It was a beautiful tiny fawn, golden and translucent, as if carved from quartz. A black arrow pierced its throat.

"You are not in a civilized place, our hunt is long over, and . . ." Perchta slapped Ginch with the flat of her sword, knocking the gallant brownie to the ground, "I can do. *Whatever. I. Want.*"

"I think not!" a deep, valiant voice declared. From out of the shadows of the library tree strode the brave and noble Sir Justinian! Just behind him trudged the good squire Grouse, leading an old, sway-backed horse laden with gear.

The Professor hopped up and down and clapped, and Shade's heart soared with hope. "Sir Justinian! What are you doing here?"

Sir Justinian smiled winningly, white teeth gleaming in the twilight. "Having lost all trace of the fearsome beast we sought—"

"*You* sought," Grouse muttered.

"My good squire and I decided to follow you, knowing that you might need our aid—"

"Because he gets bored easily."

"And sensing that, in spite of your attempts to convince me otherwise, you were on some grand quest!"

"But mostly because he couldn't think of anything better to do with his time," Grouse grumbled.

"Now leave her, vile Duchess of Sighs! In the name of the Seelie Court, I arrest thee and thy cohorts for attempted child abduction!" Sir Justinian pointed his sword at them. "Surrender, and I will take thee unharmed to the Seelie Court where thou shall receive fair trial. Resist, and feel the burning kiss of my cold steel blade!"

Lady Perchta laughed a cruel, haughty laugh. "I choose . . . *resist*." She whistled, and the riders and human goons encircled Sir Justinian and Grouse.

"Arm thyself, good Grouse," Sir Justinian said as he readied himself for combat. Grouse grabbed a heavy iron skillet from the horse. "Not with a saucepan, squire! Grab a sword."

"For the last time, this is a skillet!" Grouse barked. "The saucepan is deeper! And I'm much better—"

Not waiting for this culinary debate to play out, one of the savage humans charged, bellowing at Grouse, sword raised high above his head. Grouse swung his skillet in a wide arc that connected hard with the side of the barbarian's face. He landed heavily, spitting out teeth as he hit the ground.

"With a *skillet* than a sword!" Grouse finished.

Justinian raised an appreciative eyebrow. "Fair enough. Let's give them what for! Ha!"

Metal clanged against metal as riders and barbarians fell upon Justinian and Grouse. Lady Perchta turned her attentions back to Shade, the Professor, and

Ginch, who rubbed the bright red side of his face. "They'll make short work of your knight in tarnished armor and his surly squire," Lady Perchta purred. "As for you, little Owlet, you I will take care of myself."

As she said that, Ginch balled up his fists, and the Professor plunged his hands into his coat pockets and pulled them back out, each one sporting battered metal gauntlets. "You're-a no going to—" Ginch began to say before he and the Professor were seized from behind by the wulver, spriggan, and goblin twins. They thrashed about, but to no avail.

"So much for them." Perchta smiled her hideous, scarred smile. Shade held *Goodnight, Little Sprite* against her chest, not sure if she was trying to protect it or protect herself with it. Whichever was the case, she failed at both as Perchta snatched it from her hands and kicked her hard in the stomach. Shade fell to her knees, the wind knocked out of her.

"Give it back," she gasped.

Lady Perchta turned the book over in her hands then flipped through the pages. "Why, it's nothing but a children's book," she snorted. She looked Shade in the eyes, her own seeming to soften with understanding and sympathy. "But it means something to you, doesn't it? Something very special. I can see that it does . . . Good."

Lady Perchta tossed the book off the cliff.

"NO!" Shade shouted. *I can't lose it. Not again,* she thought, and before she knew what she was doing, Shade leapt over the cliff.

"Sprootshade!" and "Sh-sh-shade! No!" her friends screamed, but she was barely aware of their cries—all her attention was focused on the red leather book as it fell toward the dark, hungry sea below. Without thinking, Shade held her arms against her sides and her legs together and gave a few hard flaps with her wings before folding them close to her body as well. She shot down, the distance between herself and the book closing second by second. The harsh, cold waters roared louder and louder as she plunged downward. She drew nearer and nearer the book; the sea loomed larger and larger. If she waited much longer to pull out of her dive, she would hit the waters below and either die on impact or drown in minutes. In desperation, she reached out her hands. Her fingertips touched the sides of the book. Like a falcon seizing a pigeon in its talons, she grabbed the book, opened her wings, and pulled out of her dive, the toes of her boots kicking up a spray of salt water as she glided just above the tops of the waves.

It's safe! Shade exulted as she flapped her wings and rose higher. *I saved it!*

But her euphoria vanished in an instant as she re-membered where she had left Ginch, the Professor, Grouse, and the wonderful—and criminally un-derused in this story, in the opinion of your humble narrator—Sir Justinian. *My friends! That ugly, evil scab-eater has them! Somebody has to save them!*

Shade instantly knew who that person had to be. Her brow furrowed and lips narrowed in grim deter-mination. With a mighty beating of wings, she soared back up the brilliant white cliffs as the last light of day glowed on the watery horizon.

26

In which there is a good deal of
hitting, kicking, slapping and such . . .

Shade sailed up the Marble Cliffs, then soared over the heads of Lady Perchta and her thugs to land—with only a slight stumble, she noted proudly—between them and the clanging combat of the terribly outnumbered Sir Justinian and Grouse, giving her just enough space from both groups to do what she needed to do before anyone could stop her.

On seeing her, Ginch and the Professor's eyes lit up. "Sprootshade! You're alive!"

"Good," Perchta said, swooshing and slashing her sword in front of her. "I would have been so disappointed if your death were as simple, quick, and relatively painless as a quick dip in the sea. Now, Little Owlet, I believe that I shall begin by—"

"Boring me to death with inane threats?" Shade asked as she tucked *Goodnight, Little Sprite* in her backpack. "I mean, I've read much better threats in some really great books. Maybe you could steal one of those."

Lady Perchta growled and bared her perfect white teeth. "I'll begin by ripping your tongue out!"

Shade pretended to yawn as she unstrapped the thin valise from the front of her backpack. "Shudderpike used that one in *The Tragedy of Lavinia*. Pretty gruesome stuff—glad I only skimmed it. So, just curious, you're not questing for any prey anymore, right?"

"Only you," Perchta said, stepping toward her.

"Great!" Shade undid the latch on the valise. "Say, Sir Justinian? Quick question—I know you're busy, but still—you aren't looking for a quest at the moment, are you?"

"I have one! My quest—hut!—from now until—oof!—my dying day," the wonderful, very-much-deserving-of-his-own-book Sir Justinian called as he (and Grouse, I suppose) valiantly fought tooth and nail against barbarian and mounted goblin alike, "will be to see—gah!—the treachery of Perchta and Modthryth exposed and—ha!—the land finally cured of the pestilence of the Sluagh Horde forever! Yah!"

"Good plan," Shade muttered, opening the valise. "So everybody here either currently has a quest or isn't really looking for one?"

"I'd like-a to be free and get in-a the good card game," Ginch said, struggling with the spriggan pinning his arms to his sides. The Professor nodded in agreement.

"I don't think that counts, so we should be good. Hey, Glatis!" Shade yelled into the valise, backing away as Perchta stalked closer. "I need you to come out and come out big!"

"Do I have to?" a voice whined from inside the bag. "We were about to have a limbo contest."

"Yes!" Shade shouted. "Remember the grubsuckers that tried to hunt you when you were little? Well, they kind of want to kill and skin us now!"

"For starters," Perchta hissed. "I don't know what sort of trick you think you're pulling with that bag, Little Owlet, but let me assure you that—Aagh!"

Whatever Lady Perchta had planned on assuring Shade of went unassured as a thirty-foot-long creature with the head and neck of a snake (now decorated with a lovely necklace made of purple flowers), body of a leopard, and ox hooves sprang from the small suitcase and planted one of those hooves squarely in the middle of Perchta's chest. The blow sent her bowling into the wulver and the goblin that were restraining the Professor, knocking them to the ground. From the wriggling heap of fairies, the Professor sprang nimbly and struck the spriggan in the side of the head with a mighty *KLANG!* of his gauntlet.

"Oi! I'll do ya fer that, mate!" the spriggan bellowed,

letting loose Ginch with one hand to swat at the Professor. Ginch shoved his freed hand into his jacket and pulled out a deck of cards, which he arched and sent shooting into the spriggan's face.

"Fifty-two card pick-up!" Ginch laughed, stomping on the distracted spriggan's foot, then kicking him in an area far too indelicate to mention. (I'm quite appalled to even have to hint at such an ungentlemanly action!) As the spriggan's eyes bugged out and he dropped to his knees clutching the . . . area (sigh!), Ginch danced nimbly away. "Actually, sixty-three—I find-a the fifty-two make it harder for me to win."

Meanwhile, Glatisant the Questing Beast galloped at the melee where Sir Justinian and Grouse were struggling and opened her mouth to let out a "Roar!" Now you would probably assume (quite understandably) that a roar coming from a thirty-foot serpent/leopard/ox creature would be so terrifying as to freeze the blood in anyone's veins. However, Glatis, having a lovely, delicate voice that sounds, as luck would have it, very similar to your dainty Aunt Gladys's, sounded much more like someone's dainty aunt shouting "roar" than an actual fearsome beast. Rather than strike terror in any of the combatants, her roar merely made the nearest mounted goblin pause and look over its shoulder.

"Really?" the goblin scoffed. "Is that supposed to— *EEYAAAA!*"

Glatis's roar may not have scared the goblin but being chomped about the middle by a giant snake head and then tossed off a cliff certainly did. Seeing and hearing a screaming goblin soar through the air was enough to make everyone pause. Glatis took this opportunity to rear up on her hind legs, let loose with an equally unterrifying roar, and then whip her head down to exhale a mighty column of flame at two of the human barbarians attempting to lay low the brave Sir Justinian (and, I suppose, Grouse). They shrieked and flailed in a desperate attempt to put out the flames before finally madly dashing off the cliff to plunge themselves in the cool waters below.

Shade whistled appreciatively. "You never said you could breathe fire, Glatis!"

Glatis gave her a snakey smile and then belched a puff of smoke. She covered her mouth with a hoof. "Sorry. Breathing fire—*burp!*—always unsettles—*burp!*—my tummy. *BURP!* Horribly embarrassing . . ."

"Good to know."

Seeing three of their fiercest fighters fallen and the others breaking ranks and fleeing, the bear-helmeted goblin spurred his horse on to Lady Perchta's side. He reached down and swept her gracefully up behind him. Lady Perchta shrieked in frustration and glared at Shade and the rest. "I swear, on my honor as the Duchess of Sighs and on the souls of all my ancestors, I will be avenged! Little Owlet, from this day forth, you and your friends shall—"

BUUUURP! Glatis belched a massive cloud of fire. The goblin's horse just barely escaped the flames as it galloped off along the darkening cliffs.

"Disgusting!" Shade could hear Lady Perchta shouting in the distance. "Dishonorable and disgusting . . ."

Shade crossed her arms and watched them flee. "Yeah, kind of. But pretty dingle-dangle effective."

The Professor clapped his hands and raced over to Glatis, his arms held wide. She instantly transformed into a white fox and jumped into his arms. Sir Justinian limped toward them, sword still in hand.

"You know—*urp!*—that we're on the same side, right?" Glatis purred, batting her long eyelashes.

"That I do, most noble of beasts." Sir Justinian smiled broadly. "That I do."

"Okay, is everyone all right?" Shade asked, scanning the faces of her companions. She started walking back to the library tree. "Since that's settled, I need to go return a library book."

27

In which Shade returns a library book . . .

"Open up!" Shade pounded on the door in the tree. "Open up!"

The Professor walked over shaking his head. He turned the knob and opened the door a sliver before gesturing for Shade to go in.

"Oh. I didn't think to try—"

The Professor sighed and rolled his eyes.

Shade was about to push the door open then paused.

What if they don't let me come back? she worried. *I mean, I don't think* I *would let a book thief ever come back to my library. No. I've got to do this. It's their book, not mine, and they can keep it safer than I ever could. If that means I'm banished forever, then I guess I'll just have to live with that.* Shade gulped—which did nothing to settle her stomach as it twisted itself into a series of increasingly complicated knots—and pushed open the door. She was surprised to find François and Émilie standing right there at the entrance, smiling.

Okay, weird . . . Shade thought as she took the book from her bag. "Here. I'm sorry—I took this and need to give it back."

François sipped his coffee. "Mademoiselle Shade, you did not take ze book. 'E did."

Shade looked over her shoulder to see the Professor standing right behind her. He grinned and gave an enthusiastic wave. "What? But how did you—"

"Oh, we gave it to him to give to you," Émilie said.

"You gave it to him?"

"Oui. It was a test," François explained.

"A *test*?" Shade could feel her face getting hot.

"Oui! A test." François beamed. "And it is my pleasure to say zat you—"

Shade punched him in the shoulder. The gargoyle didn't flinch. Shade, however, shook her hand, then clutched it with the other. "OW! Thistleprick! Dingle, dangle, donkled thistleprick, thistleprick, THISTLEPRICK!"

". . . passed," François finished. "You know, you really should not 'it people made of ze stone."

"Really?" Shade growled through clenched teeth. When she saw that the Professor was pointing at her with his mouth wide in a silent laugh, she slugged him hard in the shoulder with her good hand. He frowned and rubbed at it. "What kind of dingle-dangle test is having him pretend to steal a book for me?"

Émilie placed a cool, smooth hand on her shoulder. "Your love of literature and learning were undeniable, and in our private conversation Professor Pinky impressed upon us your scholarship and your determination, but we needed proof that your dedication to books was greater than your own personal desire to possess them."

"So we 'ave ze test. And you pass wiz flying colors," François said warmly. "Alzough we did expect you to return ze book a little quicker. Perhaps you wrestle wiz your conscience a bit and—"

Shade swatted Émilie's hand from her shoulder. "No, I had to save it from being thrown in the ocean and then save my friends and myself from being killed by a crazy Sluagh noblewoman, who my mother apparently disfigured, and her vicious pack of killers, so I'm terribly sorry *if your dingle-dangle coffee got cold while you waited safe and sound in here!*"

François took the coffee cup from his lips and exchanged a sheepish look with the alabaster woman. "Well . . . eh . . . none of zat was part of ze plan . . ."

"Really?" Shade hauled off and hit the Professor in the shoulder again. He grabbed it and opened his mouth in outrage. "I can't hit them without breaking my hand, so I had to hit you," Shade explained. The Professor gave a resigned shrug.

François sighed and looked into his now empty cup. "Well, if you do not want ze job—"

"Oh, I'm taking the job! And if you ever pull a dingle-dangle stunt like that again, my friends and I are going to go out and get some sledgehammers and pickaxes and chisels and chip you down until you're small enough to fit on a chessboard and then we'll play chess with you. Every night. Long games. And keep you in a box when we're not playing. Get me?"

"Mais oui!" François chuckled and turned to Émilie. "Quite ze spitfire we 'ave found, no?"

"You have no idea!" Shade spun on her heel and headed back outside. "I'm going to get my friends. Find us someplace comfortable to sleep in here!"

It wasn't until she was outside that what had just happened finally sunk in.

Shade gave a little squeal and ran out to where the rest of her friends stood tending to each other's wounds. "Hey, everybody! We're going to sleep in the library—*where I now work!*—tonight! No cold winds! No morning dew! No attacks in the wee hours of the morning!"

Amid the general appreciative hubbub, the wonderful Sir Justinian raised a hand for attention. "Thank you, good sprite, but as men of combat, my good squire and I must pass, for—"

"Puckernuts to that," Grouse grumbled, grabbing his bedroll from their swayback horse. "I'm going in."

"But Grouse! We are warriors! Creature comforts—"

"Are much appreciated, especially after almost dying. Look, I've got the chance to sleep someplace warm and dry for a change, plus they probably have some really good cookbooks I can swipe some recipes from. Grouse pushed past Justinian and entered the library, calling over his shoulder, "Be sure to tell the owls and the crickets and the spiders I said, 'Buzz off!'"

"That rudeness is a clear violation of chivalric courtesy!" Sir Justinian called after Grouse as everyone else filed past him and into the library. "We will have words about it in the morning!"

Under orders from the head librarians, Caxton fetched blankets, and everyone sacked out in the great reading room. With moonlight streaming in through the immense windows there, Shade looked around. In the corner, Grouse slept slumped in a high-backed chair with *Mastering the Art of French Fairy Cooking* by Julia Anklebiter open on his lap. Ginch lay flat on his back on one of the couches, snoring under the hat covering his face. And curled up together on one of the intricately patterned rugs were Glatis and the Professor.

Tired though she was, it took Shade hours before she could fall asleep, too excited at the thought of spending the rest of her life there amongst the books and her head buzzing with too many questions.

The next morning, over a lovely breakfast of delicate, fruit-filled pastries and savory sausages (made by the booted cat, Johannes) and a delicious omelet (made by a surprisingly chipper Grouse), Shade asked the librarians: "So what if I had decided to just keep the book? Were you really prepared to lose a book from your collection for the sake of testing my character?"

"Mais non, my little butterfly," François assured her between sips of coffee. "Caxton, what time is it?"

"If oi 'adn't been swindled out o' me watch, oi'd know, wouldn't oi?" Caxton growled, his eyes throwing daggers Ginch's way.

Ginch took Caxton's watch out of his pocket. "It's-a minute to eight."

"Pop on out to ze railing and look at Johannes's desk, if you please."

Shade left the small dining hall and did as the gargoyle suggested. Shade had no idea why she was looking at the big desk with a small stack of books and a few papers on it until suddenly another small stack of books appeared out of nowhere and then another bigger one appeared and then a couple scrolls popped out of nowhere and rolled off and finally an immense tome approximately the size of the door to a sprite's house thudded on the desktop.

"One of François's ideas to make the vast knowledge of the library more available to people," Émilie explained as Shade returned to the table. "Instead of everyone coming here and poring over the books only when we keep the library open, people can now borrow the books from us. After a week or whenever readers are done with them—or if they are in danger of being damaged—they are magically transported right back here!"

Shade choked on a bite of omelet. "If they'll be damaged, they'll . . . so I didn't have to risk my life to keep that book from falling into the sea? If I had missed, it would have just popped back here?"

Johannes nodded as he passed the sausage plate so that Caxton could have thirds. "Ja, safe und sound."

Shade punched Ginch in the shoulder. "Hey! Why you hit-a me?"

Shade pointed across the table at the pixie. "The Professor's too far away to hit."

"That's-a the good point," Ginch conceded, rubbing his arm.

"And since we're on the subject of new ideas, our first assignment for you is of vital importance to our goal of making books and learning available to *everyone*," Émilie said.

"Really?" *My first assignment! This is really happening!* Shade felt giddy.

"For too long, knowledge, learning, ze arts, zey 'ave been 'idden away on far-off seashores or locked behind castle walls. Now imagine ze world we would 'ave if ev-

eryone could come 'ere and bask in ze light of learning!"
François threw his arms wide, sloshing coffee in his en-
thusiasm. "Look at yourself! Imagine, my little drought-
starved lily, 'ow you will blossom now zat ze rain of
knowledge will fall upon you every day! And imagine 'ow
enlightened ze world would be if everyone 'ad zis chance!"

As François spoke, Shade got more and more excited. "That sounds amazing! What can I do?"

"I got-a the question," Ginch said before François or
Émilie could answer Shade. "So you wanna have everybody come-a here, eh? How you think-a everybody get-a
here to the edge of the kingdom? I mean, we come-a
through the Grum Forest and we get-a attacked by the
gooblins and the Perchta and the gooblins and the rats
and the gooblins—you know, now I think-a on it, we
really get-a attacked by the gooblins a lot . . ."

"Very astute, Monsieur Ginch. That is the exact problem that we are in the process of solving," Émilie replied. Ginch smiled and hooked his fingers in his
waistcoat pockets, looking quite pleased with himself.
"The paths to our seaside paradise are fraught with peril.

So rather than have people come here, we have decided to bring here to them. Follow me, if you please."

"What do you mean 'bring here to them'?" Shade asked as they wound their way down to the ground floor. "I mean, I guess letting visitors take books from here does that a little but—"

"But zey still need to come 'ere to get zem! Precisely!" François said leading them across the grand hall to the exit door. "So we 'ave begun to open up a series of . . . *branches* to our library."

François and Émilie chuckled. "I do so love living in our metaphor!"

"Because it is a *tree*, oui?" François explained to their non-laughing guests. "We 'ave ze tree so we 'ave ze *branches* and ze *leaves* and—"

"So . . . what?" Shade asked. "You want me to help you build another library somewhere or—"

"Mais non," Émilie said, opening the exit door. "Something much more wonderful. Please step outside and you will understand."

"Okay but I don't know how . . ." Whatever Shade had

planned to say vanished from her mind when she looked out past the shade of the gigantic oak tree to see a lovely, flower-filled meadow with a small brook meandering through it. She turned around to see Émilie and François beaming from the doorway. "Where did the ocean go?"

"It is right where we left it," François said with a wink.

Émilie beckoned. "Come back and take a look at the lintel of the door you just walked through."

Shade did as she was told. There, at the top of the doorway, was inscribed "Meadowbrook." François placed a hand on her shoulder and pointed to a different door between two sets of shelves, above which it read "Marble Cliffs."

In her initial awe, Shade had not taken much notice of the several doors on the ground floor, but now she saw that each had a name carved above it. She ran across the room and went through the door marked "Mount Wyrd" to discover a craggy gray mountain stretching up into thick white clouds above. Through the door labeled "Stormfield," Shade found a dark, dismal plain over which the winds howled and dark clouds crackled with lightning. Finally, the door marked simply "Wall" opened on a little country town just beyond a quaint cobblestone wall that separated it from the copse of trees in which the library oak stood.

Shade ran back into the library. "How did you do it? How can the library be in all these places at once?"

"Why, magic, of course," Émilie answered. "Done by the same wizards, witches, and scholars who transformed our library into our lovely tree of knowledge."

"Drawing upon, I might add, ze most advanced work in applied intra- and extra-spatial studies like zat done by ze most esteemed Professor Pinky," François added. "I 'ope you are impressed, my friend."

The Professor clapped and tipped his hat to the librarians, who bowed and curtsied. François then reached into his jacket and pulled out a large acorn that he handed to Shade. "All you need to do is plant zis in ze ground and—viola!—we 'ave anozer branch and more fairies will 'ave ze chance to set zere minds alight with ze fires of learning!"

"Okay," Shade said. She didn't relish the idea of

tromping off somewhere so soon after arriving, but she was willing, if it meant a lifetime surrounded by books afterwards. "Where do you want me to go?"

"Well, as you can see, we have these three branches established, and we have volunteers currently on their way to Bilgewater, Enderby, Jeroboam, and several other places along the major rivers and coasts of the kingdom," Émilie explained. "What we don't have is anyone helping us to reach the more out-of-the-way middle parts of the kingdom."

Shade started to get an uneasy feeling in the pit of her stomach.

"Now when we 'eard zat you come from . . . what was ze name of ze—"

"Pleasant Hollow," Shade groaned.

"Oui! Pleasant Hollow in ze 'eart of ze Merry Forest."

"Which would be a wonderful place for us to establish a branch," Émilie chimed in.

Shade felt sick to her stomach. "You want me to go back to Pleasant Hollow?"

"Mais oui!"

"But it's dangerous and would take so long—"

"I can give you a ride," Glatis offered. "In my other form, I'm exceptionally fast and—"

"Yeah, great, thanks for the offer, really." Shade frowned at the helpful Questing Beast. "But Pleasant Hollow is filled with clodheads!"

"All the more reason for us to give them a chance to improve their minds just like you did," Émilie replied, gentle reproach in her soft voice.

Shade looked at Émilie and François, their faces filled with encouragement, hope, and benevolence. She wished she had a mallet and chisel. "Oh, thistle-prick!" she exclaimed, grabbing the acorn from the gargoyle's hand. She stomped to the door marked "Marble Cliffs." "I'll do it. But I guarantee this will be the rottenest branch on the library tree."

"Thank you," Émilie said.

"'Urry back," François added. "We 'ave so enjoyed your company, we 'ate to see you *leave* so soon! Heh, heh! You see, because ze trees, zey 'ave ze *leaves* and—"

"Oh, shut up!"

28

In which Shade should learn some sort of valuable, morally improving lesson, but let's not get our hopes up . . .

"You're sure you won't come with us?" Shade asked as she, the Professor, and Ginch sat on the leopard-furred back of the once again gigantic Glatis.

"Thank you for your offer, good junior librarian," the far-too-good-for-this-story Sir Justinian replied, making Shade blush with pride, "but the good Grouse and I must away posthaste to the Seelie Court. 'King' Julius may be a frivolous fool, but no doubt his advisors and wise members of the Seelie Court will see the perils posed by the Duchess of Sighs and the rest of the Sluagh menace, which you and your companions have helped reveal. Once again, thank you, good Lady Shade, for you have given me a noble quest on which to embark!" Sir Justinian took Shade's small hand and gave it a kiss.

Grouse snorted. "Yeah. *Thanks.*" He grabbed the reins of their old horse and trudged down the sloping cliffs, muttering to himself. "Least I got that crêpes recipe. And the one for boeuf bourguignon. And that one for . . ."

With a smile and a wave, Sir Justinian bade Shade and company a final farewell and jogged after Grouse, thus taking with him the last shreds of respectability this story had to cling to . . .

I'm sorry, good Reader, but would you mind terribly setting down the book for a few minutes? Maybe five.

Yes, five would be good. I just need a little time to mourn our loss here before finishing our tale.

•

Thank you. I do believe I can soldier on to the end of the book now.

•

After a long journey that concluded at the troll toll bridge, Shade set out early the next day for Pleasant Hollow. Ginch, the Professor, and Glatis all offered to go with her, but she insisted they stay with Chauncey— she felt that this was something best done on her own. So, with Chauncey reading his beloved Owlslyn, Ginch and the Professor cheating at cards, and a furry little Questing Beast snoozing contentedly in the sun, Shade took to the skies. As she fluttered and glided over the tall grasses of the plains, she remembered how long and arduous the walk had been. The little sprite that had been so insecure and self-conscious that she refused to fly even when alone now seemed like a stranger to Shade as she landed steadily on the well-traveled heels of her boots on the edge of the Merry Forest, which seemed much smaller than it had when she left.

She took out the acorn given to her by François and Émilie and looked at it for a long time. *Do I really have to go back to Pleasant Hollow?* she wondered. *Why not just plant it here on the edge of the forest? It might be easier for people to find. And it's not like any of the bug-brains back home will ever use it . . .*

"Excuse me, but can I help you find anything?" a tiny voice asked, making Shade jump. In the shade of one of the trees, a tiny figure with a tiny lantern hovered in the air.

"Anthony?" Shade smiled as she stepped towards the wisp.

"Oh, you know Anthony?" the wisp asked, zipping close enough for Shade to see that this wisp was taller and had a little beard. "Actually, I'm Abraham o' the Wisp."

"Oh." Shade took a step back and crossed her arms. "So you were about to—"

"Oh, no, no, no!" Abraham exclaimed, waving his hands. "I really was going to help you! Anthony has convinced a few of us that being helpful is the right thing to do, so that's what we do now. If you get lost, give a holler, and one of us will come flying if we can!"

But she knew there would be no need; she knew the way to Pleasant Hollow.

I'll go there, meet with Chieftainess Flutterglide, be told that they don't want it, be convinced that they are complete thistlepricks, and then go back and plant the tree on the edge of the forest, she thought as she walked. *Or maybe next to Chauncey's house. Might be nice to just step out and visit with him instead of flying an hour or so to visit.*

This was her plan until she reached the edge of Pleasant Hollow and discovered the biggest, grandest house the village had ever seen, newly built in a mighty pine. Three stories of wood polished shiny-smooth sat nestled amongst the lower branches, with a lovely porch bedecked with hanging flower pots—a perfect place to read on a summer day—right there overlooking the entire village.

They said they were going to build me a new house, but this? This is magnificent! Shade shook her head. It didn't make any sense. They had never liked her or her parents, had never made them feel welcome, didn't seem to feel that bad about burning down her house, and, quite frankly, seemed relieved when she had left. *Maybe I was wrong about them. Maybe they aren't as stupid or selfish as I thought they were.*

As she reconsidered all she had ever thought about her fellow sprites, a purple sprite with pink wings flitted above with a rocking chair, which he placed on the porch. When he turned to leave, he noticed Shade. "Oh! Lillyshadow Glitterdemalion! You're back! I . . . we . . . Hold on, let me get the chieftainess!" The fairy flew off, shouting, "Lillyshadow's back! Lillyshadow's back! Chieftainess! Chieftainess! Lillyshadow's back!"

The air was soon filled with a riot of color as a rainbow of sprites flitted and fluttered about, spreading word of Shade's return. Shade stood, arms crossed, watching the commotion and feeling unexpectedly fond of these silly, shallow, but, it seemed, ultimately good-hearted sprites. It took little time for nearly the entire village to assemble in front of the fancy new dwelling, everyone looking at her and whispering about her return, her new clothes, her new demeanor, yet none of them actually approached and spoke to her. *Probably waiting for the chieftainess to come and officially welcome me back and present me with my new house,* she thought.

Her suspicions seemed to be confirmed when the crowd parted and Chieftainess Sungleam Flutterglide strode toward her followed by her chief advisors, the elders of the village. She gave Shade's outfit a disapproving look, smiled a strained smile, and said, "You have returned to us, Lillyshadow Gliterdemalion—"

"Shade," Shade corrected her. "Just 'Shade.'"

"Well, as I was saying, Lillyshadow," Chieftainess Flutterglide continued. "We, um, we're very surprised to see you here again. You were so adamant about never returning that we—"

"Assumed I had gone off and gotten killed?" Shade suggested, arching an eyebrow.

"More or less," Flutterglide admitted.

"Well, I'm happy to say that I survived quite a few dangers, Sunny, and—"

"That's Chieftainess Sungleam Flutterglide," Flutterglide interjected.

"Oops. *So* sorry. Isn't it annoying when people don't call you by the name you prefer? Anyway, as I was saying, Flutterby, I've braved quite a few dangers, seen many amazing things, and it looks like my path has brought me back here, and I must say I'm surprised. I had no idea that when you said the village would build me a new home, that you'd make me something so big, so elegant, so—"

"Oh, this isn't your new home," Chieftainess Flutterglide said, pointing at the new house. "Once we started building, we decided, since it was a Grand Project, why not make it the grandest home that Pleasant Hollow has ever seen, which we did. And obviously we wouldn't waste such a house on someone like . . ." Shade frowned as Flutterglide searched for the right words. ". . . someone who probably would not be returning to us."

"So it's not for me," Shade said.

"No, it's my house," Flutterglide replied, proudly. "Obviously as chieftainess of Pleasant Hollow, I should have the biggest, nicest house. I was planning on moving in today."

"In that case, your old house—"

"Is going to be occupied by Head Elder Pondsparkle."

"And his house is—"

"Going to Junior Elder Raincloud. There's been a major reshuffling because of this new chieftainess's residence and—"

"And I have no place to live here, do I?" Shade said.

"Actually, the Mossgrave house is available."

"The Mossgrave house? The oldest, smallest, poorest built, most dry-rotted and termite-infested house in the village?"

"It also sustained some minor fire damage when your house burnt down. But, yes, the Mossgrave house. And we would . . . love? . . . for you to live there. If you plan on staying here, which I'm sure you don't, but . . ."

Yep, thought Shade. *This feels more like the Pleasant Hollow I know and loathe.*

"Okay, look," she said, taking out the library acorn. "You don't really want me here, and I don't really want to be here. But I've been sent by some wonderful people—I don't know *why*—to establish a library here."

Chieftainess Flutterglide frowned. "What's a 'library'?"

"It's an amazing place filled with books and information and smart people and—"

"We pass," Flutterglide said.

"What?"

"We pass, right?" Flutterglide looked at the elders, who all nodded and murmured assent. "Yes, we pass. We do not want this 'library' here. Your family and their 'books' and the 'big ideas' they used to get from them were always a nuisance. Like when your father wouldn't let us dye the pond water pink to celebrate the feast of St. Figgymigg—"

"Which would have killed all the fish and made the water undrinkable," Shade pointed out.

"It would have been so pretty! Or the time your grandfather stopped us from having a town mascot—"

"Which was a rabid bear that could have killed us all."

"Its foamy mouth looked so cute and silly!" The elders all smiled and chuckled at the memory. "And, of course, there was that time when you didn't want us to have a fireworks display—"

"Which was about a week ago, and it led to my entire house being burned to the ground!"

Chieftainess Flutterglide frowned and shook her head. "So you said, but we have our doubts. In fact, many of us are convinced that it was those horrible books that actually caused the fire."

"Wow! That may be the dumbest thing you have ever said!" Shade could feel her face getting hot. "And that's saying something because you have said some of the dumbest things in the history of dumbness. If Duke Dunston du Derdeeder ever puts out a new edition of his *Complete Compendium of Daftness, Dopiness, and Doofiness*, you should get your own chapter, Flutterbutt."

The chieftainess put her hands on her hips. "That's

Chieftainess Sungleam Flutterbutt—I mean *Flutterglide*—and I forbid you from bringing more books into this village!"

Shade looked at all the hard faces of the elders glaring at her. "You know what? When I came back here, I thought that maybe I had been too hard on you over the years. Maybe you were smarter and kinder than I gave you credit for. And now I know: You are even more stupid and selfish than I ever imagined. Honestly, you don't deserve a library here."

Shade was about to take her acorn and leave (much to the relief of most of the sprites assembled there) but then she noticed someone in the crowd. It was a boy, short and pudgy, his skin a dull gray. And there next to him stood a tall, skinny girl with drab brown wings and skin the color of moss. They were exactly the sort of sprites that would get picked last for acorn toss, if they even wanted to play.

Exactly the sort of sprites that would not realize how beautiful their coloring really was because all their brightly-colored peers would mock them relentlessly because they looked different. Exactly the sort of sprites that could find the sort of comfort and companionship and joy and inspiration denied them in their daily lives between the covers of books, just as Shade had done at their age. Only these two—and who knows how many other misfits there in the village, probably even ones that were good at acorn toss and looked just as "beautiful" as everyone else—didn't have books to get them through those sad mornings and afternoons and nights (or the happy ones and all the ones in between for that matter), did they?

Shade held her head up high and clutched the acorn in her hand. "But you know what? While most of you are nothing but pond scum-slurping, grub-gobbling, slug-licking clodheads, a few of you aren't and deserve better. And maybe if you had half a chance, some of you clodheads could stop being clodheads. So like it or not, you're getting a library!"

Shade made a small hole in the ground with her heel, dropped the acorn in, kicked dirt over the top, then dashed away. The ground began to tremble. Leaf-covered branches erupted and soared up to the skies, carried there by a massive central trunk that grew taller and taller and wider and wider as a vast root system grew deeper and snaked outwards down below, making the ground buck and furrow. At last, the library tree reached its full height, dwarfing even the largest and oldest trees of the Merry Forest and completely blocking the view from the chieftainess's new porch.

Shade walked up and opened the door to the library, then turned and faced the sprites who still remained, noting the smiles on the faces of the young sprites from before. "Library's open from sunrise to sunset, sapheads," Shade said, grinning and crossing her arms. "And there's not a dingle-dangle thing you can do about it!"

· EPILOGUE ·

In which your humble narrator is finally freed from his odious assignment . . .

O h, I do so wish I could have said, "And they all lived happily ever after!" at the end of that last chapter. Partly because I would finally be done with this dreadfully inappropriate tale, but mostly because that's how one is supposed to end stories like these. It's just what one does! But, no, the wretched writer of this story, contrary to the end, refused.

"Nobody lives happily *ever* after," the old curmudgeon grumbled when I tried to gently correct him. "If you're lucky, you live *mostly* happy after. *Regularly* happy after. But *ever* after? Nope."

So you see what I'm up against here. But I do have the following to share: At the end of our tale, Shade had a job in the library and a small room crammed full of books to call her own, from which she enlisted the services of Anthony o' the Wisp and the rest of his "Wisps of Good Will" to lead scholars through the woods to the Pleasant Hollow branch of the library. Chauncey built a lovely inn by the river where Glatis remained to sleep by the fire and protect the place, retreating into one of Chauncey's many vacations whenever a quester chanced by. The good Sir Justinian had a cause to devote himself to, which gave Grouse something to regularly complain about. And the Professor and Ginch, well, they returned to Gypsum and wandered elsewhere from there, cheating at cards and stealing whatever they could fit in their pockets (which is an awful lot in the Professor's case). I can't say that I approve of their choices, but the two enjoyed themselves immensely.

In short, all those that we have come to care about in this story were, for at least one brief moment, all happy at the same time. Such a rare and wonderful occurrence is definitely cause for celebration and perhaps the best way to conclude this, our otherwise quite dreadful, fairy book.

THE END

· ACKNOWLEDGMENTS ·

(Jon)

It would probably be impossible to thank everyone who helped bring this book into the world, so if you think you should be thanked here and aren't, you're probably right, I apologize and hope you take some comfort in knowing you aren't alone in being slighted.

First and foremost, I have to thank my wonderful wife, Nikki. She was the one who told me a couple years ago, "You should write that fairy book. Your kids are still little and might really enjoy it." She was right, as she usually is about things. I also need to thank my children, Evelyn and Jack, for listening to and reading my story, actually liking it, laughing at the funny bits, and telling me what bits needed to be funnier. So much of who I am comes from all the books I devoured and all the time I spent roaming libraries as a child, so thanks, Mom and Dad, for all you did to create and nurture my love of literature and libraries.

Outside of my family, the person most responsible for this book and almost everything else I've written is my great friend, Drew Bequette. Drew, your dedication to writing and your courage to pursue your literary dreams have inspired me, your encouragement and support have helped sustain me, and your friendship means the world to me. Thank you for everything. And thanks to Julie Bequette, their two darling children, Andy and Penny Bender, and their three darling children for being wonderful friends to me and my family and some of *Dreadful Fairy*'s biggest cheerleaders.

A lot of people were kind enough to read my little book on its long journey from first draft to print, all of whom made it better thanks to their feedback and encouragement, including, but not limited to, my dear friend and favorite poet Sylvia Cavanaugh and the Bayview Writers Group (Kristine Hansen, Lisa Kaiser, Elke Sommers, Sheila Julson, Michael Timm, Neill Kleven, and Brooke McEwen). You people are awesome!

None of my efforts, even with that overwhelming and thoroughly undeserved amount of help, would have come to anything if it hadn't been for my fantastic agent, Adria Goetz and all the amazing people at Amberjack Publishing: Dayna Anderson, Cassandra Farrin, Cherrita Lee, Kayla Church, and Joel Barton. Thank you all for making my childhood dream of some-day having a book sit on shelves in libraries come true.

Finally, I need to thank you, the readers, for taking the time to read this. I hope you enjoyed it.

—JON ETTER
THE GRAND LIBRARY, ELFAME, JUNE 2018

• BITTER RECRIMINATIONS •

(Quacksworth)

This whole narrating assignment has been such an un-pleasant ordeal, that I'd like to take this opportunity to chastise everyone that Mr. Etter has just thanked. Shame on you all for aiding and abetting this affront to all that is good and proper in children's literature!

—QUENTIN QUIGLEY QUACKSWORTH, ESQ.
QUACKSWORTH MANOR (AKA "THE QUACKSWORTHERY")
SWIFFINGTON DOWNS, BUMBLESHIRE, JUNE 2018

· ABOUT JON ETTER ·

Hailing from the great American Midwest, Jon Etter has taught in Wisconsin public schools for over twenty years. When not teaching or attempting to domesticate his two children, Jon has written tales for a number of anthologies and journals. He loved every minute of working on *A Dreadful Fairy Book* that wasn't spent with Quentin Q. Quacksworth, whom Jon describes as "the opposite of fun." For more about Jon, visit him on the web at www.jonetter.com.

· ABOUT QUENTIN QUIGLEY · QUACKSWORTH, ESQ.

In his storied, 43-year career as a professional narrator, Mr. Quacksworth has worked on many wonderful, *proper* pieces of literature, including *Nanny Pleasantry's Tales of Virtue, Inspiration, and Personal Improvement*; *Lovey Tumkins and the Pleasant and Helpful Wee Folk*; and *Honest Jim and the Do-Right Lads*, the last of which earned him the much-coveted Blabby Award from the International Academy of Narrators. His greatest regret, professional or personal, is his involvement with Jon Etter, whom he describes as "a pugnacious purveyor of puerile prose," and *A Dreadful Fairy Book*, which he strongly urges publishers, parents, teachers, and librarians to keep out of the hands of children.

· ABOUT ADAM HORSEPOOL ·

Adam Horsepool is an illustrator and animator living and working in Nottingham, UK. His favorite children's book (besides this dreadful one) is *Fantastic Mr. Fox* by Roald Dahl, and his favorite illustrator is Ryan Lang. To see more of Adam's art, visit him on Instagram @_horse_animation_.

Map of Elfame

Dinas Ffaraon,
home of the Seelie Court

The Gr

The Ghostwoods

The Ruins

Lost Lake

Stormfield

The
Ple

The Mountains of the Moon